FROM THE
NANCY DREW FILES

THE CASE: Nancy's looking for answers in a tangled case of treachery and dirty tricks on campus.

CONTACT: Ned Nickerson's entire future could rest on the outcome of Nancy's investigation.

SUSPECTS: Steve Groff—He went from a C-minus average in high school to a perfect score on the test. Was it hard work or hard crime?

Tom Mallin—He's a financial aid student who can't afford to do badly at Emerson. But was he desperate enough to steal?

Paul DiToma—Ned's frat brother at Omega Chi Epsilon has always had a problem with money. Did he find a solution by selling test answers?

COMPLICATION: Nancy faces the toughest test of all: conducting a complete and unbiased investigation . . . when the prime suspect is Ned Nickerson!

Books in The Nancy Drew Files® Series

The NANCY DREW Files™ 99

THE CHEATING HEART

CAROLYN KEENE

AN ARCHWAY PAPERBACK
Published by POCKET BOOKS
New York   London   Toronto   Sydney   Tokyo   Singapore

This book is a work of fiction. Names, characters, places and incidents are products of the author's imagination or are used fictitiously. Any resemblance to actual events or locales or persons, living or dead, is entirely coincidental.

AN ARCHWAY PAPERBACK *Original*

 An Archway Paperback published by
POCKET BOOKS, a division of Simon & Schuster Inc.
1230 Avenue of the Americas, New York, NY 10020

ISBN: 0-671-79491-4

First Archway Paperback printing September 1994

10 9 8 7 6 5 4 3 2 1

Cover art by Cliff Miller

Printed in the U.S.A.

IL 6+

Chapter

One

"NANCY! IT'S SO GOOD to see you again."

Brook Albright turned over the book she was reading as she jumped up from her desk chair.

"Hi," Nancy Drew said from the doorway of Brook's room at the Theta Pi sorority house.

"Bring your stuff in." Brook swept her clothes aside, making a clear space on one of the twin beds. "I'm thrilled you'll be staying with me for a while."

Nancy stepped into the room with the elegant dormer windows overlooking Emerson College's leafy campus. "You've got a great room this year, Brook." Nancy had become friendly with the Theta Pi sisters on previous trips to Emerson, when she had visited her boyfriend, Ned Nickerson.

"Well, now that I'm a junior I can choose my room," Brook said with a confident smile.

Nancy brushed back her shoulder-length reddish blond hair, then tossed her duffel bag on the extra bed and pulled off her yellow cotton sweater. "It sure is hot for the first of September," she said with a sigh. "Are you having any trouble planning your freshman-open-house day in this heat?"

Brook rolled her eyes. "I'll say. I've been running around like crazy when all I want to do is sit down and sip a soda."

"I'll bet the guys at the Omega Chi Epsilon house are sweltering, too." Nancy grinned, thinking of Ned. He had asked Nancy to come to Emerson to be a hostess for his fraternity's freshman reception on Saturday.

"Well, we all want to impress the freshmen," Brook replied. She paused. "I'm sure Ned must be dying to see you. After a summer of togetherness, he must really miss you now that he's back at school."

Nancy winced. She hadn't seen as much of Ned that summer as she'd wanted to, and though Ned hadn't complained, she felt bad about it. "I'm afraid I was away from River Heights a lot this summer, working on cases," she told Brook.

"That must be tough—for both of you," Brook said sympathetically. "If I had a boyfriend at home, it would be hard to leave when school started. But if I had a boyfriend here at school, I'd be dying to get back on campus in the fall. So I guess I'm lucky I'm unattached—it does make moving around much easier."

Nancy laughed. She'd always liked Brook's independent spirit. Brook was so attractive, with her wavy auburn hair and dark brown eyes, that Nancy found it hard to believe she had no boyfriend.

"Since you're so unattached," Nancy said, "why don't you join Ned and me Saturday night for the Dillon Patrick concert?"

"I'd love to," Brook said enthusiastically. "I adore his music."

"What else is going on this weekend?" Nancy asked.

"Well, there's a movie in the theater tomorrow night, and on Saturday there's a crafts fair on campus."

"Sounds like fun."

"This is a great time of year to be here," Brook said. "Classes haven't started yet. Everyone is just hanging out, seeing old friends after the summer and not worried yet about papers and tests."

Nancy checked her watch. "It's getting late. Ned will be wondering where I am. Want to walk down to the Omega Chi house with me?"

Brook hung back. "Three's a crowd."

"Oh, come on, there'll be so many frat brothers there," Nancy coaxed.

3

"Okay!" Brook gave in, slipping a bookmark into the novel she had been reading.

The two girls strolled from the Theta Pi house, a graceful white, columned mansion, to the Omega Chi Epsilon fraternity house.

On this late summer afternoon, the majestic old Greek houses lining the road were bustling with activity. From parked cars, students were unloading suitcases, boxes of books, CD players, computers, microwaves, framed posters, armchairs—all the furnishings of college rooms. Music blared from open windows that students poked out of to call to friends they hadn't seen for three months.

Three of Ned's fraternity brothers sat sprawled in lawn chairs in front of the house, drinking soda and munching tortilla chips. "Hey, Nancy Drew!" one of the guys called.

"Hi there, Jerry." Nancy smiled at Ned's pal Jerry McEntee. "I thought you were supposed to be in training for football. Are you sure chips are on your diet?"

With a grin, Jerry rolled up his sloppy T-shirt and massaged the taut muscles of his tanned stomach. "With a bod like this, I don't need a training diet," he bragged. The other two frat brothers groaned loudly and punched Jerry from either side.

Fending them off, Jerry laughed. "So, Nancy, did you bring Bess and George with you this time?" He was referring to Bess Marvin and

George Fayne, Nancy's two best friends from home. They'd visited Emerson with Nancy a few times, and Ned had fixed them up with various Omega Chi brothers.

Nancy shook her head, smiling. "Sorry—George had to play in a tennis tournament this weekend, and Bess was going to a friend's wedding. Have you seen Ned around?" she asked.

"Probably inside."

"Thanks, we'll go check," Nancy said. With waves, she and Brook headed indoors.

They paused in the large entry hall for a minute. One of the fraternity brothers was running a vacuum cleaner in the living room. He was slender but broad shouldered, with dark hair and tortoiseshell glasses. Seeing the girls, he switched off the vacuum and called out, "Can I help?"

Nancy couldn't remember meeting him before, so she introduced herself. "Hi, my name is Nancy Drew. I'm here to visit Ned Nickerson."

"Oh, hi, Nancy—I'm Paul DiToma. I'm in charge of Saturday's reception. Ned volunteered you to be a hostess, right?"

"Right," Nancy said. "By the way, do you two know each other? Brook—Paul—"

Turning to Brook, Paul's eyes widened. He awkwardly stuck out a hand to shake. "I'm not sure—you look familiar."

"I'm a Theta Pi," she explained, studying his lean, handsome face with obvious interest. "Maybe we've met at a mixer?"

"I doubt it," Paul said hesitantly. "I kind of avoid those parties. Everything seems so . . . set up."

"I don't go to many of them, either," Brook replied. "Maybe we've had a class together, then."

Paul snapped his fingers and grinned. "American Lit Two Twenty-one, Professor Ford," he said. "You always sat in the front row. You carry your books in a red backpack, right?"

Brook blushed and smiled. "Right. And you were always in the back corner, with your chair tipped back and your feet on the windowsill. I didn't recognize you without your leather bomber jacket."

Paul smiled shyly. "Yeah, I love that jacket. But it's kind of hot to wear it today."

"Then I'll just have to recognize you by something else. Your glasses, perhaps?" Brook ventured with a giggle.

Nancy tactfully broke into their conversation. "I'd better let Ned know I'm here. Paul, have you seen him?"

Paul turned back to Nancy. "Let me buzz his room," he offered, parking the vacuum. He walked over to the intercom and pushed a button.

Jerry and the other two guys walked in the front door, carrying the folded-up chairs under their arms. "Hey, DiToma!" called out the heavier of the two guys. He put on a high, fluty voice and continued, "I'm waiting for you!"

Nancy noticed Paul's face grow red. "Cut it out, Rich," he protested.

Jerry explained the joke to Nancy and Brook. "Paul got a note today in the *Emersonian,* in the personal ads. It said, 'Paul DiToma: I'm waiting for you.' We figure it's got to be from some secret admirer."

Paul flinched, obviously embarrassed. "Come on, guys, it's as much a mystery to me as it is to you." He quickly changed the subject. "Ned doesn't seem to be answering, Nancy. Want me to look around for him?"

Just then the phone by the front door rang. Rich sprang to pick it up. "Might be your secret admirer, Paul," he teased as he picked up the receiver. "Hello, Omega Chi . . . Hey, Nickerson! Perfect timing—your girlfriend just showed up looking for you. . . . What?"

Nancy watched as Rich's expression changed, and her instinct told her that something was wrong. She reached for the phone, but Rich held on, nodding. "Okay, I'll tell her. Catch you later." He hung up abruptly.

"What's the matter?" Nancy asked.

"I'm sure it's no big deal," Rich assured her. "But Ned's over at Dean Jarvis's office. He wouldn't say what was going on. He just asked you to meet him there."

7

Nancy nodded. "I'm on my way." She turned to Brook. "Sorry to run off like this."

"No problem," Brook said, stealing a sideways glance at Paul. It was clear she wouldn't mind staying on to talk to him. "I'll see you back at my room."

Nancy walked swiftly out the door, trying hard to believe that Ned wasn't in trouble. Ned was a star athlete and a popular campus figure, with lots of friends and good grades. He wasn't the type to give school officials a hard time.

She quickly crossed the campus, heading for the ivy-covered administration building.

When she arrived, the dean's assistant recognized Nancy from her previous visits to Emerson when she had helped crack some difficult cases. "Hello, Nancy," she said. Nancy thought she could detect a note of uneasiness in the woman's voice. "Ned said you'd be meeting him here. Could you wait outside the office? There's a bench over there."

As Nancy sat down, she glanced at the half-closed door of the dean's office. She could glimpse three figures inside. Dean Jarvis, a bear of a man, was sitting at his large wooden desk. She recognized Ned's tall, broad-shouldered back as he stood facing the desk.

She could also see the back of the third figure, another man. "But I tell you, Dean, there was only one copy," he was saying loudly and somewhat hysterically.

8

"Now, Professor Tavakolian." Nancy immediately recognized Dean Jarvis's resonant voice. "You said it was locked up in your file cabinet—"

"Yes, and the only time I unlocked that cabinet was on Monday—when Nickerson was in the room," the professor continued shrilly. "And then again yesterday, Wednesday, to take out the test. Otherwise, my cabinet was locked up tight. But when I went there this morning to get the answer sheet it was missing! He *must* have stolen it!"

Then Nancy heard Ned's voice, sounding baffled. "Why would I want to steal the answers for a freshman English placement test?" he asked. "I'm not a freshman, and I've already taken the first-year literature course. What good could it do me to get exempted from it now?"

The professor snorted loudly. "Don't think that I don't know the sort of foul play that goes on around a college campus," he replied scornfully. "True, you don't need the answers to help yourself. But," he continued in a low, angry voice, jabbing his finger close to Ned's face, "there are lots of freshmen who might have been desperate to see the answers to that test. I believe you stole the answers and sold them. Believe me, Ned Nickerson, you're not going to get away with it!"

9

Chapter

Two

Nancy's heart began to race. She knew that Ned was honest. How dare this professor accuse him of stealing anything!

"Let's not jump to any conclusions, Professor," Nancy heard Dean Jarvis say. "I can personally vouch for Ned's integrity." Then his voice went on in a soothing murmur, and Nancy couldn't make out his exact words.

The professor gave a loud *hmmph!* "I don't know this young man from Adam," his voice whined. "I only asked him to photocopy that test!"

Nancy still couldn't hear the dean. She leaned forward on the bench, straining to catch his reply.

"That's easy for *you* to say!" the professor exploded. "The test is tainted now. I'll have to start all over again. I'll have to create a new exam that the freshmen will have to take again. Then I'll have to grade it—and all before classes start on Wednesday!"

"But we're not sure anything was stolen," the dean put in. "Just because you can't find your answer sheet . . ."

"Dean Jarvis," the professor said haughtily, "I am beginning to suspect that academic integrity is of no importance to this office. Do you, or do you not, intend to take action in this case?"

Nancy couldn't stand by another minute. She hopped up and stood in the doorway. "Hello, Dean Jarvis!" she said brightly. Out of the corner of her eye, she saw Ned's handsome, square-cut face. He was flushed, whether with anger at Tavakolian or pleasure at seeing her she couldn't tell. She flashed him a swift pretend-you-don't-know-me look and he understood immediately.

"Why, Nancy Drew—" the dean said awkwardly.

"I happened to be on campus, and I thought I'd drop by to see you," Nancy said breezily. "Got a mystery for me to solve?"

The dean continued to stare at Nancy in confusion. She swiveled around and got her first good look at the professor. He was a man of medium height with a chunky build, curly pepper-and-salt hair, and a neat black beard. Despite the hot weather, he wore a rumpled tweed silk jacket over a dark blue polo shirt.

"Sorry—was I interrupting anything?" Nancy asked innocently.

Dean Jarvis cleared his throat. "Professor Tavakolian, this is Nancy Drew," he said. "She's a talented detective who has helped us solve a number of mysteries on campus."

Nancy shook hands with the professor and then turned to Ned and stuck out her hand. "Nancy Drew," she said, introducing herself.

Ned's dark eyes sparkled with amusement and relief. "Ned Nickerson," he said quietly, trying hard to keep a straight face. As they shook hands, Nancy could see the dean's baffled expression.

"A detective, you say?" the professor asked. "Well, it just so happens we do have a problem. Someone has stolen the answer sheet to an important exam." He removed a handkerchief from his pocket and mopped his brow, then quickly replaced it.

Nancy glanced at the dean, and she saw understanding dawn in his eyes. "Professor, perhaps you'd like to tell Nancy your story."

"I would indeed," the professor declared, then quickly retold the story Nancy had already heard. Nancy nodded and listened thoughtfully.

"I'd like to go to your office to check out the scene of the crime," she suggested when he had finished.

"Excellent." Tavakolian beamed. "If you'll excuse us, Dean?"

"By all means," the dean said. But as the

professor headed out the door, Dean Jarvis pulled Nancy aside. "Are you sure you know what you're up to, Nancy?" he whispered.

"Thanks for not blowing my cover, Dean Jarvis," she whispered back. "Maybe I can find out if the test was actually stolen or not."

The dean nervously glanced at the professor waiting outside the door. "Nancy, I don't want any complaints about a conflict of interest. You must investigate quietly—Tavakolian doesn't know Ned is your boyfriend, but lots of people at Emerson do. And after all, Ned is our chief suspect."

"But . . . but I thought you said that you didn't believe Ned did it." Nancy frowned.

"I can't afford to take anything for granted," the dean replied. "Can I trust you to pursue this truthfully, no matter where it leads?"

"You can, sir," Nancy promised, shaking his hand. Then she glanced over at Ned, who was still standing awkwardly by the desk. Their eyes met only for an instant, but they knew each other so well that an instant was all they needed. Without a word, she knew he trusted her, too.

Drawing a deep breath, Nancy turned and joined the professor in the hallway. They headed for Ivy Hall, an old brick classroom building in the center of campus.

"I'm an English professor," the professor told Nancy as they walked. "I teach one of Emerson's core curriculum courses. All Emerson students have to take four courses before they graduate—a world history course, an earth sciences course, a math and computer course, and a literature course, which is the one I teach.

"I said all students have to take the courses," he added, "but there are exceptions. During orientation week, freshmen take placement exams in those four subjects. If a student scores well on a specific test, he or she can skip that required course and get extra credit for it."

"And it's the answers for that test you think were stolen," Nancy said.

"I *know* were stolen," Tavakolian corrected her. "On Monday afternoon I asked the English department office for a student aide to photocopy the test. Apparently all the student aides in the English department were busy, so the department secretary, Ms. Belzer, called the campus jobs office to send over a temporary worker."

"Ned Nickerson," Nancy filled in.

Tavakolian nodded as he held open the door of Ivy Hall for her. "I had a single copy of the test and the answer sheet on Monday afternoon. I handed Ned the test and asked him to make two hundred copies of it."

"You gave him the test only?" Nancy asked.

"Yes. I left the answer sheet in the file folder, with the computer disk containing the test and the answers," he replied firmly. "While Ned went to make the copies, I placed the folder on my desk.

"When he brought the copies back," he went on, "I put the original copy of the test back in the folder. I laid the folder aside for a minute when I was putting the photocopies in my file drawer. That's when I think Ned stole the answer sheet. Then I put the folder in my file drawer and I left my office, locking the door."

"When did you return next?" Nancy asked.

"Yesterday morning, Wednesday, at ten-thirty," he said. "I picked up the copies and took them to the auditorium, where the test was scheduled for eleven o'clock."

They were walking down the second-floor hallway when the professor abruptly stopped outside a varnished wood door. F. M. TAVAKOLIAN was painted on the door in flaking black paint.

"Was this door locked yesterday when you got here?" Nancy asked.

"Of course it was." The professor pulled out a small key ring, attached to his leather belt by a short chain. "My keys are always with me, you see," he noted as he slipped a key into the lock and pushed open the door. "No one 'borrowed' them, if that's what you're thinking."

The professor ushered Nancy into his small, book-crammed office. He gestured toward a tall black steel cabinet next to his battered wooden desk. "The file cabinet was locked when I got here, too."

"Did you notice whether the answer key was in the file yesterday morning?" Nancy inquired.

Tavakolian huffed slightly. "Well, no—I didn't check inside the folder Wednesday morning. All I needed were the tests to hand out to the students. I took the completed tests home with me last night, and I didn't return until this afternoon, when I came to get the answer sheet."

"Were the office door and the file cabinet locked this afternoon when you got here?" Nancy was closely studying the surface of the file cabinet, looking for scratches that might indicate someone had jimmied the lock.

"Yes, definitely," Tavakolian answered as he took out his key and unlocked the cabinet. "I kept the test folder in the bottom drawer."

Nancy opened the deep bottom drawer of the cabinet and glanced over the folders crammed into it. "Aren't you going to dust for fingerprints?" the professor inquired curiously.

Nancy hid her annoyance at his meddling. "I doubt that that would help us here," she said politely. "A surface like this is probably covered with many people's prints. Besides, we're not looking for a criminal whose prints would be in a police file. Now, do you still have the original copy of the test?"

From the drawer, Tavakolian pulled out a ten-page document on plain white copy paper from a manila folder. Nancy held it up to the light to study the typeface. "I took my disk and printed the test out on the laser printer in the

English department office," the professor said. "It's faster than my printer here."

Nancy nodded, rapidly checking out his desktop computer setup. Then she scanned the test itself. "If someone cheated on the test, he or she would get a high score, right?" she asked.

"Well, you see, there are two sections of the test," Tavakolian pointed out. "The first part is multiple-choice, with fifty questions—the answers are A's, B's, C's, and D's. Whoever stole the answer sheet would get a perfect score on that part. But the second part of the test wouldn't be easy to cheat on." He flipped the pages to show her. "It consists of five essay questions."

"And the answer sheet didn't list answers for essay questions," Nancy concluded.

Tavakolian shrugged. "For each essay question, I did write down a few phrases, indicating topics that should be covered by the student. But when I grade such a test, I also give points for clear, intelligent thinking."

"So we might be able to identify the cheater," Nancy mused, "if a student gets a perfect score on the multiple-choice section and mentions the correct topics on the essay questions, but doesn't really seem to understand them."

"True," said Tavakolian.

"Although the only clear proof of the theft would be to find the missing answer sheet in a student's possession," said Nancy. "But if you had the tests graded, we could zero in on the most likely cheaters."

"I hadn't planned to grade them at all," Tavakolian said, "since the test has to be thrown out. But if you wish, I will grade it. I'll do the multiple-choice section first.

"Of course," he added fussily, "it will take me a number of days to correct the essay section. In any case, I'll give you the names of any students who get a perfect score on the multiple choice."

As Nancy jotted down her phone number at the Theta Pi house for the professor, she asked, "Does anybody else have a key to this office?"

"No. Oh, there's the cleaning woman," he remembered, "but she doesn't have a key to the file cabinet. Besides, she barely speaks English. What use could she have for a literature exam?"

About as much use as Ned Nickerson would have, Nancy thought to herself. "I'd like to speak to her anyway," Nancy told him.

"I think she starts work, down the hall, around now," Tavakolian said. "I'll see if I can find her." He went out the door.

While he was gone, Nancy conducted a careful inspection of the office. First she searched through the other two drawers of the file cabinet. The professor seemed to have a well-organized filing system, she noticed. Each file had a neatly typed label and was in perfect alphabetical order.

Next she moved to the large double-sash window that overlooked Emerson's central lawn. The glass rattled loosely in the wood frame, but the old brass lock fit tightly. No one had climbed up to the second floor and entered that way.

Stepping over to the office door, Nancy inspected the lock there. It was a cylinder lock, set into the wood. She recognized the brand name and knew it was a good, sound lock, almost impossible to pick. It didn't seem as though anyone had broken into the office.

Just then the professor returned, leading a middle-aged woman with graying blond hair. Over her slacks she wore a flimsy mustard-colored smock. Her deep-set blue eyes reflected her fright.

Nancy offered her a seat, but the woman shook her head and stood beside the chair. As Nancy gently questioned her, she said her name was Sophie Maliszewski. She'd worked at Emerson for twelve years, ever since coming to the United States from Poland. Showing Nancy her large ring of keys, she said that she cleaned the professor's office every weeknight, usually between seven-thirty and eight.

"The professor says something's missing from his office—a piece of paper," Nancy said.

"The professor have many piece of paper here," Sophie joked weakly.

Nancy smiled. "We think someone may have stolen the answers to a test."

"And if there was cheating going on, the students will have to take the test over again," Tavakolian said.

Suddenly Sophie's pleasant round face went absolutely white. "Oh, no!" she cried out, greatly agitated. She collapsed into the chair beside her, and her head fell forward. Nancy rushed to her side. Sophie was about to faint.

Chapter
Three

SOPHIE GAVE A WEAK PUSH to Nancy's arm, indicating that she would be all right. Nancy stepped back and watched the woman closely, wondering why she had reacted so strongly. Two or three seconds went by, then Sophie lifted her head and stared at the wall in a daze.

"What did you say?" Nancy asked her gently.

Sophie shook her head. "I am sorry. I just—I feel sorry for the students, they work so hard, to take this test a second time . . ."

"Do you know something about the missing test answers?" she pressed.

Sophie shook her head with vigor. "No, I know nothing. I never see any paper."

"I believe her," the professor said quickly. "Sophie, you go on back to work. Thanks for talking to us."

As soon as the woman was out of earshot, Nancy turned to the professor. "Professor, you were the one who wanted this incident checked out," she reminded him. "I'd appreciate it if you wouldn't interfere with my work."

Tavakolian reacted with surprise. He clearly expected all teenagers to be in awe of him. "I wouldn't dream of interfering," he said. "But don't you think you ought to interrogate Ned Nickerson? He is our prime suspect, not this poor laborer."

Nancy stifled a smile. "Yes, I agree. I'll go interview Ned Nickerson right now."

"Good," the professor nodded. "Now, if you'll excuse me—I have a lot of tests to grade."

After saying goodbye to the professor, Nancy walked back to the Omega Chi Epsilon house, hoping to find Ned. As she expected, he had gone back there and was waiting for her in the living room.

"Let's go to the downstairs study lounge," Ned suggested as he took her arm. "No one'll be there today, and we can talk."

They passed through the living room into the lounge and sat down on a lumpy green sofa. "I can't tell you how good it is to see you, Drew," Ned said, his dark eyes gazing into hers. "When you walked in the dean's office, I felt frustrated, having to pretend I didn't know you. All I wanted was to take you in my arms—like this." He slid his arm around Nancy's shoulders, drew her to him, and gave her a long kiss.

Nancy's insides melted as she surrendered to the kiss. But halfway through it she surprised even herself by pulling away.

"Remember what the dean said," she whispered softly as she drew away. "I can't let our relationship influence my investigation."

Ned brushed her comment aside. "I'm not worried—I know I didn't take that answer sheet," he murmured, lips brushing her cheek.

"So why don't you tell me your side of the story?" she said.

Ned reluctantly straightened up and began his version of events. "Okay—Monday afternoon. The English department secretary, Ms. Belzer, called and asked me to go to Tavakolian's office. He handed me the test to photocopy. I went down the hall to the English department's photocopier."

"You went straight there?" Nancy asked.

Ned nodded. "Yeah. But then, while I was at the machine I saw that one page of the test was missing. I went back to ask the professor where it was, but he wasn't there."

"Where was he?" Nancy asked.

"I don't know." Ned shrugged. "I figured he was coming right back, because his computer screen was still on. Then I noticed he'd left the manila folder he kept the test in right on his desk.

23

I looked inside it for the missing page, but all I saw was the answer key and a computer disk."

Nancy frowned. "So the answer sheet was there then," she said. "What did you do next?"

"I figured the disk had the test on it, so I took it back to the English department office," Ned continued. "Ms. Belzer let me boot it up on her computer. I printed out the missing page, then took the disk back to the professor's office. He still wasn't there, so I put the disk back in the file folder."

"And was the answer sheet still there then?" Nancy checked.

Ned nodded. "Then I went back to the copier and made the copies. I took them to Tavakolian —he was back in his office by then. I handed him the stack of copies, which he then put in the bottom drawer of the cabinet. That's when I left."

"So Tavakolian doesn't know that you used his disk with the test on it," Nancy mused.

Ned looked nervous. "What difference would that make? The answer sheet is what's missing."

"True," Nancy agreed. "But if the professor knew you'd borrowed his disk, he'd be even more convinced that you're guilty. We can't clear you until we find out where that answer sheet went."

"And how do we do that?" Ned asked.

Nancy leaned forward, her elbows on her knees, frowning. "That's the part I haven't figured out yet," she admitted.

An hour later, after Nancy and Ned had had a chance to chat and catch up, they decided it was time to get something to eat. As they went out the front door of the frat house, Paul DiToma came sauntering down the stairs behind them. "Hey, Ned! I see you found Nancy," Paul called out.

"Yeah, thanks, Paul." Ned turned, grinning.

Paul said to Nancy, "Going to meet Brook?"

Nancy looked confused. "Did she say she was expecting me?"

"Not that I know of," Paul said, and Nancy noticed the slight blush on his face. "I was just asking."

"Oh, so you know Brook?" Ned asked.

"I just met her today," Paul explained, following them out the door. "It's funny, even though we're both English majors, we never got to know each other before. Does she, uh, have a boyfriend?"

"No, not right now," Nancy said.

"Come on, Paul, go for it—ask her out," Ned urged his friend. This time, Nancy saw the blush deepen to scarlet.

"Ned and I were heading for the snack bar—want to join us?" Nancy asked.

Paul considered for a moment. Digging a hand inside his pocket, he pulled out a couple of crumpled one-dollar bills and some loose change. "Better not tonight," he said. "I don't want to spend any more money until the weekend.

Thanks, though—some other time." He waved goodbye and set off in another direction.

Ned and Nancy went on to the student center, a large, old-fashioned stone building that had once been the home of the university president. "I like Paul," Nancy said as they sat down with their burgers at the far end of the main room where tables were clustered. "He's a refreshing change from all the jocks in your frat."

Ned playfully punched Nancy's arm. "Hey. I'm one of those jocks."

"You know what I mean," Nancy said with a smile. "Should I warn Brook about him?"

"No, Paul's a decent guy," Ned assured her. "He doesn't date much. He's kind of shy, around girls *and* guys. It would be great if he and Brook got something going."

"What about the personal ad addressed to Paul that was in the *Emersonian* today?" Nancy asked. "Jerry and Rich were teasing him that it was from some girl."

Ned shrugged. "Who knows? Hey, Jerry and Rich might even have put in the ad as a joke."

"I'm not so sure. Maybe I should call the newspaper office tomorrow to find out who placed the ad," Nancy mused.

"Nan, you've already got one mystery to solve —don't go inventing new ones."

"Oh, you know me—one mystery is never enough," Nancy said good-naturedly.

Ned reached up under her red-blond hair and ran his fingers lightly along the nape of her neck. "I think I can find a way to get your mind off mysteries for the evening," he said in a husky voice.

"Promise?" Nancy asked, her blue eyes shining.

"Promise," Ned replied.

Before breakfast the next morning, Nancy met Ned on the Theta Pi lawn and they went jogging around the campus lake. "Out of shape, Drew?" Ned teased her as they pounded up the final slope.

"No way, Nickerson," she retorted cheerfully. "Want to do another lap?"

Ned laughed and slowed to a walk. "Sure, I could handle it. But I have to stop by the library to sign up for a study carrel—a private cubicle in the book stacks. I want to make sure I get one near the political science books. Do you mind if we swing by there now?"

Nancy agreed, and they walked up the hill to the library, a new building with walls of shining reflective glass. After Ned filled out a carrel request form, the librarian gave him the number of his carrel. Ned led Nancy down into the underground book stacks where his carrel was situated.

The stacks were long, low-ceilinged, windowless rooms, with rows of bookshelves on each side of a center aisle. "I've never seen so many books in one place," Nancy said, marveling.

"Some students are complaining that we need a new library wing already," Ned told her. "The library was crowded practically from the day it was built. So they installed these sliding bookshelves to store more books in the limited space."

He pointed to long lines of gray steel shelves on each side of the center aisle and perpendicular to it. Ned grasped a handle on one and cranked it. It moved slowly forward, shoving a stack of other shelves forward. A space opened between the shelf Ned was pushing and the one behind it. Each bookcase sat on wheels, which rolled along two steel tracks the length of the center aisle.

"If I wanted a book on this shelf, I could slip in and get it now," he said, pulling out a book at random. "Of course, who'd want to read about Sumerian archaeology?"

Nancy laughed. "I'm sure somebody does, and that person is glad the library made room for these books."

Leaving the library, Ned and Nancy returned to their houses to go to their rooms to shower and dress. Reaching Brook's room, Nancy found a message on the answering machine from Professor Tavakolian, asking her to call him. She dialed his number quickly.

"Well, I stayed up late last night grading the

tests," Tavakolian told her. "I'm only halfway through, but I've already found three perfect scores—more than usual."

Nancy grabbed a scrap of paper. "Why don't you give me the students' names?" She jotted them down as the professor spelled them out: Carrie Yu, Gary Carlsen, and Steve Groff. Then Tavakolian rang off, after promising he'd call her later with any more names.

Looking up the three students in Brook's new campus directory, Nancy phoned them. Introducing herself as Professor Tavakolian's assistant, she set up appointments to interview the first two students at the professor's office— Carrie Yu at eleven o'clock, Gary Carlsen at eleven-thirty.

But when she talked to Steve Groff, Nancy immediately sensed trouble. "Why do you need to interview me?" Groff asked. "All this orientation stuff is taking up too much time. I came here on a swimming scholarship. If Emerson wants me to swim, why don't they let me get on with it? I need to spend all day training at the pool."

"Then I'll meet you at the pool in twenty minutes," Nancy suggested quickly. "It should only take five or ten minutes. You'll recognize me—I've got red-blond hair and I'll be wearing a white T-shirt and dark blue running tights." She hung up before Groff could object.

After a brief phone call to Ned to tell him she'd meet him for lunch, Nancy grabbed a raisin-bran muffin from the Theta Pi kitchen and sprinted over to the sports center, an enormous complex on the far side of campus. The pool was in a large room with one glass wall overlooking the football field. Nancy sat on the bleachers beside the empty pool, watching the locker-room door. Soon a tall, tanned guy with huge shoulders and chlorine-bleached short hair walked out in his trunks.

"Steve?" Nancy called out hopefully.

The guy looked up at her.

"Hi, I'm Nancy Drew," she said, standing up. "I called you earlier."

The swimmer stared at her belligerently.

"Professor Tavakolian tells me you did quite well on the placement test," Nancy continued. Steve's eyes flickered, but he said nothing. "I just wanted to ask you how you studied for the test, and what your high school English teachers taught you to prepare for it," Nancy pressed on, improvising her story.

Steve snorted. "My high school teachers did nothing to prepare me for it. They were jerks—I taught myself everything."

"That test covered a lot of material," Nancy said guardedly. "How did you know what to study?"

"I read a lot, okay?" Steve replied, snapping his towel. "Just because I'm a jock, you think I can't read? Hey, what is this really about?"

Nancy decided to risk showing her cards.

"There was a question about whether a copy of the test answers leaked out," she began.

"Oh," Steve interrupted, beside himself with fury. "And you jumped to the conclusion that I cheated?" His eyes flashed with a nasty gleam, the veins in his forehead protruding. "Well, I'm sick and tired of being sold short. Let me tell you, Nancy Drew, you'll be sorry if you don't get off my back!"

Chapter
Four

NANCY DREW BACK in surprise, but she quickly regained control of the situation. "I'm interviewing several students about the test," she told Steve calmly. "Perhaps you saw somebody else in the room cheating?"

"If I did, I wouldn't tell," he snarled. Wheeling around, he dove into the pool, splashing water on Nancy. With a resigned shrug, Nancy left the sports complex, her T-shirt damp but not worth changing.

Glancing at her watch, Nancy saw it was almost time for her next two interviews. She headed for Ivy Hall.

Professor Tavakolian was at his desk in his office, surrounded by stacks of test papers. He suggested that Nancy use a study lounge down the hall to interview the students. Nancy waited outside his office until Carrie Yu arrived, exactly on time. Carrie was a short, stocky girl with blunt-cut black hair and gold-rimmed glasses. Nancy greeted her and led her to the lounge, a small windowless room with a few scruffy armchairs and low tables.

"The professor says you did quite well on the test Wednesday," Nancy said as they sat down.

Carrie's face lit up. "Really? Good enough to be allowed to skip the course?"

Nancy tried to be noncommittal. "I think so, but the professor will let you know for sure."

"I hope so," Carrie said. "I'm a pre-med student, you see, and I could use the extra class time for a science course."

"You shouldn't have trouble getting into med school if your grades are good," Nancy noted.

"They're pretty good," Carrie said. "At least in math and science. English and history aren't my best subjects. . . ." She stopped, as if she wished she hadn't admitted her weak points.

"Unfortunately, there's a chance that some people may have cheated on the test," Nancy said, closely watching Carrie's reaction to this news.

Carrie's face remained blank. "Really?"

"The professor may have to throw out these scores and retest you all," Nancy added.

Carrie pursed her mouth stubbornly. "That's a drag. I just hope I do as well next time."

Nancy realized she wouldn't get anything more

out of Carrie Yu. After a few more routine questions, she finished the interview and walked out to meet Gary Carlsen.

Gary was a skinny, nerdy guy with close-cropped black curls, thick glasses, and medium-brown skin. As he sat in the lounge with Nancy, he answered her questions with a cynical smirk.

"That test was a pushover," he scoffed. "The Chaucer quotations were translated into modern English, when everybody knows Chaucer wrote in the Middle English dialect. And there wasn't a single question about metaphysical poetry."

"English is a favorite subject of yours, I see," Nancy prodded.

"Oh, not just English—I also read German, French, Russian, and Spanish literature. And I plan to take classical Greek here at Emerson. But physics and astronomy are my real loves. Those and ancient history."

"And Sumerian archaeology?" Nancy threw in.

"Oh, do you study Sumerian archaeology?" Gary asked eagerly.

"No," Nancy admitted wryly. "Did you happen to see anyone cheating on the placement test?"

Gary gave a short, scornful laugh. "I didn't pay much attention to the other students. I finished the test early and went back to my dorm."

After Gary left, Nancy sat for a while thinking. Having copies of her suspects' high school records to tell which students were brains and which ones weren't would help.

Nancy decided to go down the hall to the English department office, three doors away from Professor Tavakolian's office. The only person there was Ms. Belzer, the motherly-looking secretary, sitting at her computer at a large desk just inside the doorway. "Oh, yes, Nancy Drew," she said with a smile when Nancy introduced herself. "Mr. Tavakolian told me you'd be using the lounge."

"May I use your phone for a minute?" Nancy asked. Ms. Belzer nodded and turned the phone toward her. Nancy made a call to Dean Jarvis, who promised to arrange for her to get access to student records in the admissions office.

Then Nancy asked Ms. Belzer to show her around the English department office. The secretary pointed out the faculty members' cubbyholes for mail and a large bulletin board with several sign-up lists and notices on it. The department's laser printer sat on a table near the windows, behind a bank of file cabinets. Through an archway was a small side room, where the photocopier was.

"Do you remember Monday afternoon, when Ned Nickerson was photocopying Professor Tavakolian's literature test?" Nancy asked the secretary. "He used your computer to print something out."

Ms. Belzer knit her eyebrows. "Gee, Monday

was a real zoo around here, with all the freshmen coming in. I just don't remember. People are always borrowing my computer, because it's hooked up to the laser printer. Have you seen how fast that gizmo can print out a document? It's awesome, as the kids would say."

Just then, Professor Tavakolian walked in. "Ms. Drew, I'm glad I caught you," he said. "Believe it or not, I've graded the rest of the tests. Speedy grading—that's the main virtue of multiple-choice tests, isn't it, Ms. Belzer?"

"Whatever you say, Mr. T," said the secretary cheerfully. Nancy could sense her affection for the professor.

"I have three more students who made perfect scores," he announced. "Usually there are only one or two perfect scores. Now we have a total of six—highly suspicious, I'd say."

He handed Nancy a slip of paper with three more names written on it: Tom Mallin, Annie Mercer, and Linda Corrente. Ms. Belzer handed Nancy a copy of the new campus directory, and she began phoning the students.

Answering Nancy's call, Annie Mercer said she was just going out the door. "I don't know if I'll have time to meet with you today," she said breathlessly. "There's so much going on. I'm signed up for a tour of the library at one-thirty, and at three I have tryouts for field hockey, and then I'm going to the bookstore—"

"We could do it sometime over the weekend," Nancy offered. "I'll be around."

"Oh, but I'll be busy then, too," Annie hurried on. "My roommate and I are going to the crafts fair to buy stuff for our dorm room, and there's the concert Saturday night."

"How about if I meet you at your dorm room, Saturday at twelve-thirty?" Nancy offered.

"Y-yes," Annie said reluctantly.

"See you at twelve-thirty." Nancy hung up.

The other two students agreed to meet Nancy at the professor's office that afternoon—Linda Corrente at three o'clock, Tom Mallin at four.

Before meeting Ned for lunch, Nancy had just enough time to go to the admissions office one floor below Dean Jarvis's office. The admissions director, Ms. Karsten, called Dean Jarvis to get clearance for Nancy to look in the admissions files, much of which was confidential information. Once she got his approval, Ms. Karsten showed Nancy an enormous metal file cabinet, where copies of each freshman's application materials—SAT scores, high school grades, application forms, and teacher recommendations—were kept in thick green file folders. Nancy pored over her suspects' files intently. Three of her suspects looked like shoo-ins for perfect scores: Gary Carlsen and Annie Mercer were both straight A students, and Linda Corrente, a gifted poet, did well in English.

The other three didn't have stellar records in English. Carrie Yu had A's in math and science, but C's in history and English. Tom Mallin's English grades were mostly B's, and Steve Groff's were C's and D's, though his high SAT verbal score suggested some untapped ability.

Nancy was still mulling over this information as she rushed into the student center five minutes late. "Sorry—I got held up," she apologized to Ned, dropping a kiss on his cheek.

Ned rolled his eyes. "Nan, you're still in your running clothes from this morning!"

"I know." She grimaced, glancing down at her white T and blue running tights. "I'll shower and change after we eat, but I'm starving—let's get in line."

Ned followed her, groaning. "Nan, I was looking forward to having the weekend with you. Are you going to spend the whole time on this case?"

"I hope not," she said. "But, Ned—I'm just trying to clear your name." She smoothed the sleeve of his light blue cotton shirt, hoping he'd understand.

"I know, I know." He waved his hand. "Did you find out anything interesting?"

Nancy hesitated, peeking back over her shoulder. "I can't say yet—most of what I learned today is confidential."

Ned acted hurt. "You mean I can't even help you with the case?"

Nancy bit her lip. "There's one thing you could

do—call the *Emersonian* and find out who placed that personal ad to Paul DiToma."

Ned was obviously perplexed. "Okay—but what does that have to do with the missing test answers?"

"Nothing, probably—I'm just curious," said Nancy. She picked up a tray and peered into the glass food case. "Oh, good, tuna salad plate!"

After lunch Nancy ran back to the Theta Pi house, showered, and changed into fresh clothes —black jeans and a mint green cotton sweater. As she walked back to Ivy Hall, she went over her list of six suspects—especially Carrie Yu, Steve Groff, and Tom Mallin, whose perfect scores on the test were suspicious.

Linda Corrente was waiting for Nancy on a chair outside Professor Tavakolian's office. She had long chestnut brown hair, slanted gray-blue eyes, and a smoky soft voice.

As soon as she and Nancy were seated in the lounge, Nancy told her about the stolen test answers. Linda acted shocked, but she was only mildly concerned when Nancy said she might have to take a new test. "If I did well before," she murmured, "I'll probably do well again. Anyway, I don't care whether I get exempted from the course. I love taking literature classes." Nancy nodded, mentally striking Linda off her list.

Since her interview with Linda was over so quickly, Nancy waited in the hall for Tom Mallin. When he finally came, he was walking hesitantly. He had a round, fair-skinned face and china blue eyes. Nancy introduced herself and led him to the lounge. She noticed that he darted nervous glances around as he perched on the edge of an orange armchair.

Nancy told him about the stolen test answers and the possible new test. "Another test? What if I don't pass it next time?" Tom asked anxiously. "I studied so hard for it the first time. I might have forgotten everything by the time I take it again."

"Why is it so important to you?" Nancy asked.

Tom dropped his gaze. "Well, you see—I'm on financial aid. I'm afraid my money may run out before I can get my degree. Any extra credit I can pick up will help."

Nancy felt sorry for him, but she steeled herself. The question for her was, did passing the test mean so much to Tom that he'd cheat? She asked him several questions about his whereabouts on Monday afternoon and on Wednesday morning, and made notes to check his alibis.

Exhausted from her sessions in the stuffy little lounge, Nancy tried to clear her head as she strolled to the campus bookstore. Ned was waiting outside, sitting on a stone wall with a tall stack of books beside him. Nancy kissed him lightly. "Mmmm," Ned murmured warmly. "So —any new developments?"

Nancy shook her head as she sat down next to

him. "I'm no nearer solving the mystery than before. I have too many suspects, and there's not a scrap of physical evidence yet."

"It'll happen," Ned said, reaching out to massage her shoulder reassuringly.

Nancy rolled her head, enjoying his strong touch. "Did you go to the *Emersonian* office?"

"Yeah—what a waste of time," Ned said. "The guy who runs the personals column doesn't keep records of who placed which ads. I told Paul—I ran into him in the bookstore. He was surprised that I was checking on the ad."

"You didn't tell him that I'm a detective, did you?" Nancy asked with some concern.

"No, I know you like to keep a low profile," Ned said, winding up her shoulder massage with a friendly squeeze. "Anyway, I asked him to go with us to the movie tonight. Maybe you could invite Brook, too."

"Doing a little matchmaking, Nickerson?" Nancy teased.

"Maybe," he answered, smiling.

"Fine with me," Nancy said. "So did you get all your books?"

"At last," Ned said. "I spent three hours in that place! The lines were humongous. But I saw lots of people I hadn't seen in ages, and I had a couple of good conversations, catching up on news."

Nancy reached over and picked up a thick textbook from the pile. *"Principles of Geology?"*

"It's supposed to be an easy course—nicknamed 'Rocks for Jocks.'" Ned grinned. "I need one easy course."

"Could I look?" Nancy asked curiously. She opened the book cover and a sheet of paper fell out. Her eyes grew wide.

Across the top of the page were printed the words *Freshman Literature Placement Test— Answer Key.*

Chapter

Five

NANCY FELT HER stomach sink. The missing answer sheet—in Ned's possession!

"What's that?" Ned asked innocently.

Without a word, Nancy showed him the sheet of paper. She watched Ned's face go white.

"But . . . but . . ." Ned spluttered. He swallowed and began again. "I never saw this paper. I just bought the book ten minutes ago."

Nancy looked at him with a troubled gaze. "How could it have gotten into this book?"

"I took the book off the shelf about an hour ago, just after I finished talking to Paul," Ned recalled. "But I spent some time looking for other books I needed. I did set down my pile a couple of times while I was talking."

Nancy nodded. "So someone could have

slipped it into your book. But why would anyone do that?"

Ned looked anxious. "Someone must be trying to frame me."

"Yes, but who—and why?" Nancy pointed out. "I know you're innocent, Ned, but I have to tell Dean Jarvis and the professor about finding this. It'll put you under stronger suspicion, I know, but I can't suppress evidence."

Ned agreed, reluctantly, and walked Nancy to the Theta Pi house. Nancy called the dean to tell him about the answer sheet Ned had found. Jarvis asked to meet her and Ned at his office the next morning, along with the professor.

"Hey, earth to Nickerson!" Brook teased Ned that evening. Ned, Nancy, Paul, and Brook were sitting in the auditorium in the student center, waiting for the movie to start.

Ned, who had been staring absently at the blank movie screen, shook his head. "Sorry, Brook," he said. "What were you saying?"

"She was mocking the fine cuisine we had tonight at the Omega Chi house." Paul said with a grin.

"Come on, Paul, you have to admit the fried chicken was a little greasy," Brook teased back.

Nancy smiled, but she was acutely aware that Ned, sitting to her left, hadn't been himself all evening. She reached over and took his hand, giving it a comforting squeeze.

"So what are we seeing tonight?" Paul asked.

Brook had picked up a page of notes distributed by the Emerson Film Society. "It's a sixties detective movie called *Marlowe,*" she said, reading the sheet. Paul leaned over to read it, too. Nancy saw he was using this as an excuse to lean against Brook's shoulder.

Feeling a tug on her hand, she turned to exchange a smile with Ned. He had noticed the attraction between Paul and Brook, too.

Nancy leaned against Ned's shoulder. "Are you okay?" she asked softly.

Ned heaved a small sigh. "I'm not anticipating seeing the dean tomorrow."

"Don't worry, Ned. We'll find out who's framing you," Nancy said confidently, when she actually didn't feel so sure. She hadn't made any headway on the case yet—and she had no idea what move to make next.

The next morning at ten o'clock Ned and Nancy met the dean and the professor at the dean's office. Dean Jarvis was a different man in his weekend clothes, a knit sport shirt and Bermuda shorts. Professor Tavakolian wore his usual tweed jacket, but this time over a black polo shirt.

Nancy described how she and Ned had found the paper in Ned's book. Dean Jarvis frowned as he listened. "What do you have to say for yourself, Ned?" the dean asked when she had finished.

Ned spread open his palms. "I'm mystified. I swear I don't know how the sheet got in there."

Nancy cleared her throat. "We haven't established that the paper I found is the missing answer sheet," she pointed out.

"Well, I happen to have made a new copy of the answer key," Tavakolian replied, pointing to his well-worn black leather briefcase. He rooted around for a minute and pulled out the test, handing the top page to Nancy.

Nancy laid it on Dean Jarvis's desk next to the paper she had found in Ned's textbook. All four of them silently studied the two sheets of paper. Both sheets showed the same string of A's, B's, C's, and D's.

"There, it is the missing sheet," Tavakolian exclaimed in triumph.

The dean was concerned. "I have to say I wasn't convinced that there had been a theft at all. But now it seems clear that *someone* really did steal the test answers."

Ned swallowed tensely. "But it wasn't me!"

Nancy interrupted, trying to sound calm and objective. "It doesn't make sense, Dean. Why would Ned carry the sheet around with him after the test was over? It seems more likely that the thief—whoever it is—knew that Ned was under suspicion and planted the answer key on him in the bookstore, while he wasn't paying attention."

Dean Jarvis sighed and turned to Ned. "I won't take action against you until we have more concrete evidence. But frankly, it doesn't look good. If you did steal and sell the answers, Ned, I'd have to suspend you—or even expel you."

Nancy spoke up. "I've got six other suspects— Steve Groff, Carrie Yu, Gary Carlsen, Annie Mercer, Linda Corrente, and Tom Mallin."

The dean frowned. "Tom Mallin?"

"Why? Do you know anything about him?" Nancy asked quickly.

The dean pursed his lips. "I, uh, know who he is. But I know nothing that would incriminate him. The other names aren't familiar to me. You go ahead with your investigation, Nancy, but I hope you come up with something soon."

Ned and Nancy left the dean's office, worried and subdued. Ned reminded Nancy that he had to go help the Omega Chi brothers prepare for that afternoon's reception. Knowing that the Theta Pi house would be a madhouse, Nancy picked up a quick lunch at the snack bar before her last suspect interview.

At twelve-thirty Nancy knocked on Annie Mercer's door. A cute, bubbly girl with dimples and short ash blond hair opened the door. "Hi, Debbie," Annie said.

"Sorry—my name is Nancy, not Debbie," Nancy reminded her.

"Whoops!" Annie giggled. "Well, anyway, come in. Our room is a total mess, though—we still haven't fixed it up. Me and Claire, my roommate. I think it's so cool being at college, don't you? Do you have a boyfriend?"

Nancy was surprised that Annie seemed like such an airhead. Her high school record had shown all A's and loads of awards and extracurricular activities. Still, Nancy reasoned, she could act like an airhead in order to be popular.

"Yes, I have a boyfriend," Nancy answered, then changed the subject. "I just wanted to ask you about the literature test last Wednesday. Did you think it was too easy or too hard?"

Annie rolled her eyes. "Oh, it was easy. But I love English—it's my best subject. My boyfriend's an English major. What's your major?"

"Um, psychology," Nancy fibbed. "Did you happen to see anyone cheating?"

"On the test?" Annie asked in surprise. "Gee, no. Who would do that?"

Remembering that Annie was a straight A student, Nancy decided to rule her out as a suspect. She made up a few more questions, then left the girl's room.

What next? Nancy wondered in frustration. It was clear that she wouldn't get any information from her suspects through direct questioning. But maybe I could find some clues in their dorm rooms, she thought. She went downstairs to a phone booth and looked up her suspects' addresses and copied them into her pocket notebook.

Annie was still in her room, so Nancy couldn't begin by searching there. But Steve Groff, the swimmer, lived in Jenkins Hall, which was nearby. Nancy knew Jenkins Hall well. Ned had lived there his freshman year. It was only a short walk.

Nancy tried to act casual as she climbed the stairs to the fourth floor of Jenkins Hall. Steve Groff's room was 408. Nancy found the door and gently tried the knob. It had been left unlocked. She knocked, then pushed the door open gingerly. No one was inside.

The small dorm room, with its white painted cinder-block walls, was a study in contrasts. One side was neat and clean, with a smooth bedspread on the bed and a few books lined up on the bare desk. The other side was a pigsty. The narrow bed was unmade, dirty clothes were thrown on the floor, and empty soda cans lined the windowsill. Nancy stepped closer to the desk on the messy side. Behind a stack of dog-eared books—mostly poetry and philosophy—were two swimming trophies with Steve Groff's name on them.

Nancy knew she had to hurry—the unlocked door probably meant that Steve or his roommate had only stepped down the hall for a minute. She pulled open a desk drawer and saw several spiral notebooks, well scribbled in. It'll take me ages to hunt through all this, Nancy thought.

Just then she heard a step at the door. "What are you doing?" a voice demanded angrily.

Nancy whirled around to see Steve Groff in the doorway. He recognized her at once. "You—the English department snoop!" he accused.

Nancy thought fast. "This is *your* room?" She pretended surprise. "I was looking for, uh, Brad. Sorry!" And she slipped past him, out the door.

Steve must have believed it was an honest mistake, because he didn't follow her. Hurrying down the stairs and out the dorm, Nancy scolded herself for having been so obvious. She had learned something, though. Steve wasn't just a dumb jock. All those books and notebooks showed that he was truly interested in literature. Maybe his high test score really was legitimate.

Sitting on a grassy slope across from the dorm, Nancy took out of her pocket the list of addresses she had jotted down. Dean Jarvis had reacted oddly to Tom Mallin's name, she remembered. Maybe Tom's room should be searched next.

Tom wasn't in a dorm. He lived off campus— 1107 Uncas Street. Nancy walked over to the lot where she had parked her blue Mustang. She remembered that Uncas Street was about two blocks away but it was a long street, stretching far away from campus.

Once in her car, she followed Uncas Street, noting that the addresses at first were much higher than Tom's. She followed the street for about ten minutes, getting farther and farther from campus. The neighborhood gradually changed to small, old, shabby houses, with peeling paint and hanging shutters.

Nancy drove slowly to catch the house numbers. She was close to Tom's house now—1113, 1111, 1109—1107.

Nancy parked across the street. Tom Mallin's house was better kept than most—a square brown-brick bungalow with yellow wood trim. Beside the front steps, someone had planted a few chrysanthemums.

A light was on upstairs and an older-model brown sedan was parked in front. After her last experience, Nancy decided to wait until she was sure the house was empty before making her search.

As she sat in the car, she wondered why Tom lived here. Few Emerson students lived off campus, and those who did usually were juniors or seniors. Was Tom a "townie"? If so, it didn't look like the family had enough money to send a son to a private college like Emerson. Then, too, Tom had said that he was on financial aid.

Just then the door opened, and Nancy sat up in astonishment. Out walked Sophie Maliszewski!

Holding her breath, Nancy watched Sophie climb into the old brown car, her mind racing.

Maybe Sophie was Tom's landlady, Nancy thought. Or vice versa—maybe Sophie rented a room in Tom's house. Or maybe she had just been visiting Tom for some reason. At any rate, a connection between the two had been established. It had to mean something!

As Sophie started her car and drove away, Nancy did the same. Sophie turned at the corner onto a main thoroughfare. Nancy followed her, trying to be unobtrusive, but there weren't many cars around. After a couple of blocks, Nancy saw Sophie look anxiously into her rearview mirror, as though she'd spotted Nancy. Sophie, obviously nervous, began to drive faster.

Nancy saw that the light at the next intersection was red, but to her surprise, Sophie sped up. She's going to run the light, Nancy realized.

Nancy was determined not to lose Sophie, but she didn't want to put herself in danger.

The light turned green just as Sophie hurtled into the intersection, and Nancy sped up to follow in her wake. A large green truck on the cross street had illegally moved into the intersection and had to skid to attempt to stop. Abruptly swerving to miss Sophie's car, it came screeching straight at Nancy!

Chapter
Six

SLAMMING ON HER BRAKES, Nancy twisted the steering wheel just enough to swing her car out of the path of the truck. With a blast on his horn, the truck driver continued through the crossing, jolted over a curb, and then roared away.

Nancy pulled over to the curb and sat for a moment, gripping the steering wheel tightly. As soon as her pounding heart had slowed down, she looked up to see which way Sophie Maliszewski had gone.

The brown car had stopped on the far side of the intersection. Sophie jumped out and ran over to Nancy's car, her round face expressing her concern.

Nancy leaned out of her window. "I'm okay, Mrs. Maliszewski," she said. "How about you?"

"That truck came so close!" the woman gasped.

"Yes, we're both very lucky," Nancy said. "But why didn't you slow down when that light was still red?"

Mrs. Maliszewski looked ashamed. "I thought you were following me. I was scared."

"Well, I was following you," Nancy admitted. "But I only wanted to ask you some questions."

"You asked me questions the other day," Mrs. Maliszewski said, shifting her feet nervously. "What more do you want to know?"

"Well, for one thing," Nancy said, getting out of her car, "I want to know what your connection is to Tom Mallin."

The cleaning woman twisted her hands anxiously. "Tom? Is he in trouble? Please, he's a good boy. He don't do anything wrong."

"He got a very high score on that literature test," Nancy said, leaning against her car.

"But that is not wrong!" the woman protested. Her lack of fluency in English clearly frustrated her. "It's good to win on tests. Me, I not very good reading and writing, but I see him study hard for that test. I so upset the other day to learn Tom must take test over again. So upset. I see him study for it so hard. I see him lose many nights of sleep. He could get sick. Why you causing trouble for my son?"

"Your son?" Nancy asked. "Tom Mallin is your son?"

Mrs. Maliszewski sighed. "Tom and I left Poland after his father died. Tom, he go to school in America. The other kids have trouble spelling this Polish name, so Tom makes up a name, Mallin. He even go to court to make it his real name. For me, it's no matter. But Tom, he's an American boy. He wants an American name."

"I see," Nancy said thoughtfully. "But Dean Jarvis didn't tell me—"

"Dean Jarvis is very good to Tom," Mrs. Maliszewski said. "He help Tom get a scholarship to Emerson College, since I work at college. He knows Tom don't want everybody to know who his mother is—the woman with the mops and buckets." She turned away sadly.

Nancy's heart went out to the woman. She felt pretty sure that Sophie wasn't the thief, but that didn't clear her son.

"One more question," Nancy said. "You have a key to Professor Tavakolian's office on your key ring. Do you take it home with you at night?"

Mrs. Maliszewski nodded. So, Nancy thought, Tom might have gotten into the office that way.

Nancy thanked her for her time and apologized again for following her. Mrs. Maliszewski got back in her car and drove off. Nancy headed back to the campus.

Approaching the main lawn, she saw that the crafts fair was in full swing. She found a parking space at the far end of the oval and got out of her car.

Fifty or sixty booths had been set up along the circular paved path. A jazz ensemble played on a small makeshift stage in the center of the lawn. A comic juggler was doing his act on the steps of Ivy Hall, and a pair of mimes in black leotards and white makeup were performing.

As Nancy stood watching the juggler, she caught sight of Annie Mercer on the far side of the crowd gathered around him. Now would be a good time to search her room, Nancy thought. She left the crowd unobtrusively and quickly made her way to Annie's dorm.

Nancy expected Annie's roommate to be out, too, but just in case, she decided to knock before entering. "Come in!" a voice called out to Nancy's rapping.

She pushed open the door to see a girl with dark, curly hair sitting in the corner, where the twin beds were placed in a cozy L. "I'm looking for Annie," Nancy said.

"She's at the crafts fair," the girl said. "I'm meeting her there in a few minutes—I'm just waiting for a phone call. I'm Claire, her roommate." The girl smiled.

"I'm Nancy," Nancy said, introducing herself. "I can come back some other time. I just wanted to borrow a book."

"One of her textbooks?" Claire asked. "I know she went to the bookstore yesterday afternoon and bought a whole bunch." She gestured toward a stack of books on the desk by the brightly curtained window.

As Nancy hesitated in the doorway, the phone rang. Claire, who was sitting right next to it, snatched up the receiver eagerly. "Hello, Kevin?" she answered brightly.

Seeing that Claire was distracted, Nancy stepped over to the desk very casually. She studied the books in the stack, quickly thumbing through each one in search of loose papers.

A yellow spiral notebook also lay on top of the desk. The cover was written all over with various doodles, names, and phone numbers. Nancy riffled through it but saw only handwritten pages —nothing like a printed answer sheet.

With her back to Claire, Nancy eased open the top desk drawer an inch or so. Inside were nothing but bottles and jars of cosmetics. Odd, thought Nancy—no pencils or pens.

Looking up, she glanced at the wall above the desk, where a bulletin board hung between two posters of hunky TV stars. It was covered with a calendar, photos, old ticket stubs, and other souvenirs. As Nancy stared at it, she heard Claire hang up the phone.

"Is that Annie's boyfriend?" Nancy asked Claire, fishing for information. She pointed to a picture of a girl and boy posing beside a beat-up white van.

"No, that's Annie's sister and *her* boyfriend,"

Claire answered, coming over to stand beside Nancy. "Rona looks just like Annie, doesn't she? They're twins. No, to tell the truth, I haven't met Annie's boyfriend yet, even though he is here at Emerson. He's from her hometown. I wish my boyfriend were at Emerson—I really miss him."

"What's Annie's boyfriend's name?" Nancy asked.

Claire giggled. "I forget. She always talks about him, but I tune it out. Anyway, I have to go meet her now. Can I give her a message?"

"Oh, no—she may not remember who I am. We only met this morning," Nancy said.

"That's typical Annie. She's kind of spacy, isn't she?" Claire smiled.

"She seems that way," Nancy agreed. After thanking Claire, Nancy left Annie's room and took the stairs down one flight to Carrie Yu's room.

She knocked several times on the door but there was no response. Glancing up and down the hall to make sure that no one was watching, Nancy took out her lock pick. A few deft thrusts tripped the tumblers inside the knob, and the door opened.

Carrie's room had the same square layout as Annie's, but the effect was totally different. Carrie and her roommate kept their beds on opposite sides of the room. A tall bookcase stood between their two desks, creating separate study areas.

Carrie and her roommate had chosen a muted color scheme—navy blue bedspreads, a charcoal gray carpet, and a bank of carefully tended houseplants that filled the window. On the walls, they had placed large study charts—the periodic table of elements and a cross section of the human anatomy.

Nancy could tell right away that searching this room should be a snap. These girls seemed to be the sort who never left anything out of place.

Nancy did a quick but efficient sweep of the room. The books in the bookcase were all science texts. Their notebooks were all new and blank. The desk drawers were neatly organized, with fresh pens, markers, pencils, erasers, and paper clips stored in little plastic trays.

Nancy then moved to the two built-in dressers next to the pair of closets just inside the doorway. The clothes in the drawers held no surprises— clean blue jeans, plain light-colored T-shirts and sweatshirts.

She searched the closets next. By checking the address tags on the suitcases on the upper shelves, Nancy could tell which closet was Carrie's. Otherwise, there was virtually no difference. Neither girl had many clothes hanging up. A few pairs of shoes were lined up on the closet floor. Thinking of her friend Bess Marvin complaining about her crowded closet, Nancy had to smile.

Then, just as she was about to close the door of

Carrie's closet, something caught Nancy's eye. She bent down to look closer.

A tiny yellow scrap poked out from under one of Carrie's white sneakers. Nancy picked up the shoe. A small square of yellow memo paper was stuck to the rubber sole by its adhesive edge.

On it, in close, tiny handwriting, was a series of capital letters: B, D, C, A, A, C, B, D, C, D, A, D, B, A, C.

It looked like the answers to a multiple-choice test!

Chapter

Seven

NANCY WISHED she had a copy of the answer key with her. How could she quickly find out whether these letters corresponded to the test answers without contacting the professor?

Then she remembered that earlier that day Dean Jarvis had handed back to Ned the sheet of answers found in his textbook. She'd meant to ask him for it after they'd left the dean's office. I'll go get it right now, she decided, pocketing the yellow slip. She left Carrie's room, flicking the door lock back on as she went out.

Glancing at her watch, Nancy realized that it was almost three-thirty. The Omega Chi Epsilon party started at four! Feeling guilty, she hurried downstairs and jogged back to the Theta Pi house. The bathrooms were full of Theta Pi sisters getting dressed for their open house, but

Nancy managed to find an empty shower. She changed in record time, and left a note for Brook, arranging to meet her at six-thirty.

Wearing a simple off-white dress with her hair skimmed back into a ponytail, Nancy walked briskly over to the Omega Chi Epsilon house. The afternoon sunlight made dappled patterns as it played through the trees lining Greek Row. The weather was no longer so oppressively hot and Nancy was excited that Ned and his friends would have a perfectly gorgeous evening for their party. Arriving breathlessly at the Omega Chi Epsilon house at five minutes to four, she saw Ned detach himself from the cluster of frat brothers standing around.

"Nancy, I was worried you wouldn't make it," he said anxiously. Nancy admired how his olive green jacket and yellow shirt set off his dark good looks. Glancing at his square clean-cut chin and warm brown eyes, she thought she was the luckiest girl at the party.

Nancy smiled. "I wouldn't let you down like that, Nickerson," she said, slipping her arm through his. Looking around to make sure no one was listening, she murmured, "And I've got good news—I may have found our thief!"

Ned's eyes lit up with relief. "Really? Oh, Nan, that's fantastic!"

"But I can't be sure," she cautioned him. "I need to look at that answer key we found."

Ned nodded and ran upstairs to his room. A minute later he came back down with the sheet of paper. Carrying it over to a corner, Nancy compared it to the yellow slip of paper from Carrie Yu's room. She found the same sequence of letters, a third of the way down the answer key.

"She must have copied the answers onto two or three small pieces of paper to take into the auditorium with her," Nancy thought aloud.

"Who?" Ned asked.

"Carrie Yu," Nancy answered. "I found this in her room. It isn't conclusive proof, but maybe I can use it to force a confession out of her."

"Aren't you going to call the dean?" Ned asked. "It might get Tavakolian off my back."

Nancy was reluctant. "Accusing someone of a crime is a serious thing," she pointed out. "You know how you felt when you were accused. This slip of paper is such slim evidence. First let me confront Carrie in person. I'll call and arrange to meet her."

Ned stood behind Nancy as she called Carrie from the phone on the front hall desk. A group of freshmen were milling about on the porch as she dialed. She ducked her head to hear the phone's ringing over the noise of hearty male voices. Carrie's line rang and rang, but no one picked up.

Hanging up, Nancy turned to Ned and shrugged. "She's not in." Ned groaned, and Nancy patted his arm sympathetically. "Don't worry, I'll try again later. Let's just concentrate on the party. Show me where I'm supposed to work, okay?"

Ned led her to a nearby table just inside the front door. As the freshmen came in, he explained, she was supposed to ask their names and write out name tags for them.

For the next two hours a steady stream of freshmen poured through the door. Some stayed for only ten or fifteen minutes, then drifted on to other frat houses. Others stayed for an hour or more, trying hard to impress the Omega Chi brothers. Though the faces began to blur together, Nancy made an effort to smile at everyone graciously. She knew how important this party was to Ned. Though the formal fraternity rush wouldn't take place until February, many guys were already deciding which house they wanted to join or pledge.

A couple of times Nancy caught Ned's eye across the crowded room, and they traded smiles. Then someone would steer Ned away.

Around five o'clock, Paul dropped by Nancy's table with a glass of punch. "How are you holding up?" he asked.

"I'm getting writer's cramp from all these name tags," Nancy admitted, grinning. "But it's great that you guys attracted such a crowd."

Paul nodded. "On a different subject," he continued in a low voice. "Ned invited me to come to the concert tonight with you and him. I understand that Brook will be coming, too."

Nancy laughed and was about to tease Paul, but she was interrupted when she saw someone familiar out of the corner of her eye—Steve Groff. He was shouldering his way through the crowded doorway. With his athletic build, he looked constricted in his navy blazer and red tie.

"Name, please?" Nancy asked when he reached her table.

Steve barely looked at her at first. "Groff. *G-R-O-F-F*. Steve Groff," he said brusquely.

Nancy bent her head and copied his name onto a name tag sticker. As she handed it to him, their eyes met and he did a double take. "You again," he snorted. "What are you doing, tailing me?"

Paul leaned forward. "Can I help you?" he asked, trying to distract Steve.

Steve focused on Paul and his expression became less guarded. "Didn't I meet you at the English office the other day?" he asked gruffly.

"Oh, yes, I remember," Paul said, taking Steve by the arm. "I'm Paul DiToma. Can I introduce you around?" He led Steve away.

Nancy kept an eye on Steve and Paul as they crossed the room together. Nancy couldn't hear their conversation over the hubbub, but she could hear the tones their voices took. She could also tell a lot by watching their faces. Paul was feeling annoyed, but tried to speak to Steve pleasantly. Steve made one short, sarcastic reply. Paul winced and answered Steve coolly.

Boy, this Groff guy is really spoiling for trouble, Nancy thought to herself.

Steve stood a good three inches taller than Paul, and he was at least twenty-five pounds heavier. As their strained conversation built into an obvious quarrel, he used his physical advantage to intimidate Paul, leaning over and jabbing his finger against Paul's chest.

Nancy twisted around in her chair, looking for help. The Omega Chi brothers were on guard for situations like this. She saw Jerry and Rich close in on either side of Steve. Each guy took an elbow, and they steered Steve calmly toward the door, before he could disrupt the party.

At the door Steve twisted around for a parting shot at Paul. "Hey, Mr. Intellectual Snob! You think I'm not good enough for your lousy frat? I wouldn't join Omega Chi if you paid me! You wait until I tell folks what I know about *you.*"

Jerry and Rich gave Steve a final heave out the door. Arms crossed, they stood casually on the steps, preventing him from reentering.

Nancy jumped up and left the table to go to Paul's side. "Are you okay?" she asked.

Paul gave his head a shake and then looked at her. "I'm fine." He smiled weakly. "You think I'd let a crude jerk like that get to me?"

As Paul slipped away through the crowd, Nancy thought he had been shaken by what Steve had said. What had they been arguing about? she wondered. What did Steve mean when he threatened to "tell" people about Paul? Could this have any connection to the anonymous ad in the *Emersonian?*

By six-thirty the last guests had left the Omega Chi house. As the cleanup committee chased the stragglers out, Ned, Paul, and Nancy went out to meet Brook on the lawn.

The four young people walked across campus to the student center for dinner before the Dillon Patrick concert. By now, the weather had changed dramatically. A cool breeze had sprung up, the first sign of fall. Brook shivered in her short-sleeved dress, and Paul took off his leather bomber jacket and draped it over her shoulders.

"I met a friend of yours at our open house, Paul," Brook mentioned, snuggling into his jacket.

"Really? Who?" Paul asked.

"Annie Mercer," Brook replied.

Nancy perked up. She couldn't let on that she knew Annie—neither Brook nor Paul knew about her investigation. Still, even though she thought she'd caught her thief, she might learn something useful about another suspect—especially if more than one student had cheated.

Paul was frowning. "Annie Mercer? Oh, yeah, I remember her. I saw her over at Ivy Hall the other day, but I couldn't remember her first name. I just remembered she was one of the Mercer twins. They were two years behind me in high school."

"She has a twin?" Brook asked. "I only saw one girl at our party."

"Oh, the other twin didn't come to Emerson," Paul said. "I think she went to Yale."

So both sisters seem to be brains, Nancy thought.

"Well, anyway," Brook said, giving Paul a sideways glance, "I got the impression that she knew you real well. But when I said I'd be seeing you tonight, she shut up and walked away."

Paul shrugged. "That's weird. I remember her as super friendly."

Nancy noticed the slight tightening of Brook's features. She guessed that Brook was trying to figure out whether Paul had any old girlfriends hanging around. Nancy could sympathize with that. But Nancy was interested in other sorts of secrets, and for the second time that day, she wondered uneasily if Paul was hiding something.

"Speaking of weird behavior," Nancy said, "what was Steve Groff so mad about, Paul?"

"Oh, he's just a guy with an attitude," Paul said. "I saw him at the English office the other day, trying to talk his way into Professor Mc-Carty's American lit course. McCarty told him no way, that he had to take the core course first. Groff was embarrassed. I was standing right there, so I tried to explain to him what a tough course American lit would be without the core course as background. Somehow, he took it as an insult—like I was saying he wasn't smart.

"When I saw him this afternoon, he blew up at me," Paul said. "He said I was trying to discourage him from joining the frat because his grades weren't high enough. As if I knew anything about his grades. I barely know the guy!"

"Groff—one of the coaches mentioned his name to me," Ned recalled, holding open the door to the student center. "He's supposed to be a hotshot swimmer. I know a lot of athletes are supersensitive about being labeled as dumb jocks, but it sounds like this guy really goes overboard."

Inside, the grill was full of the preconcert crowd. Brook hung Paul's jacket over the back of a chair to claim a table, and the two couples joined the food line.

As they stood in line, Nancy peeked over Paul's shoulder to see Steve Groff enter. "Paul, it's Steve Groff," she warned in a low voice.

Steve had already spotted Paul and, with a hostile sneer, he strode toward him. Paul turned, confused, but Ned stepped forward first.

"Hi, Steve," Ned said evenly, reaching out to shake Steve's hand. "I'm Ned Nickerson. Coach O'Casey told me to look out for you."

Steve halted, surprised. "He did?"

"Yeah. I'm sorry I didn't see you at the open house," Ned said smoothly. "I hope we can talk in February, when the real rush season starts."

Steve nodded. "Okay, see you then," he muttered. He stood around awkwardly for a moment, then turned and headed off to mingle.

"Nice going, Ned." Brook smiled.

Ned grinned back. "Who knows—he might make a good frat brother, if he calms down. I don't want to judge him until I have all the evidence." He shot Nancy a glance full of meaning.

Nancy smiled back. She knew what Ned meant —he understood her reasons for not accusing Carrie Yu. She reached out and squeezed his hand.

Carrying trays full of food, the two couples headed back to their table. Brook set her tray down and leaned over to pick up Paul's jacket, which had fallen from her chair onto the floor.

Brook handed the jacket to Paul and he started to hang it on the back of his chair. Then his jaw fell open and his eyes widened in panic.

"What's wrong, Paul?" she asked.

Silently Paul held up his leather jacket. In thick black felt-tip marker, someone had scrawled THIEF all across the back!

Chapter

Eight

GAZING AT PAUL's damaged jacket, Nancy immediately thought of Steve Groff. Though Ned seemed to have diffused the argument between Steve and Paul, maybe Steve had only pretended and this was his way of getting back.

Nancy scanned the crowded room. Steve had been wearing a gray sweatshirt and jeans—the same as several other kids in the room. His distinctive chlorine white hair was nowhere to be seen.

"Steve Groff has vanished into thin air," Nancy declared.

Paul was still staring at his jacket, clearly sick at heart. "It's ruined!" he groaned.

"Maybe the writing will come out," Brook suggested, leaning over to study the brown

71

leather. "Or you could have the leather dyed darker, so the writing wouldn't show."

Looking up at his friends, Paul gave a feeble grin. "Man, that'll teach me not to spend so much money on one dumb piece of clothing."

"Don't be so hard on yourself," Ned said kindly. "You don't throw money around."

"I haven't *got* any money to throw around," Paul exclaimed. "I have to save every dime, so I can take next year off to write a novel."

Nancy noticed Brook's eyes shining with admiration. Nancy had to wonder, though, if Paul needed money so badly, how far would he go to get it? Was that why the graffiti on his coat said *thief?*

"I was just thinking, Paul," Nancy began. "First those personal ads in the *Emersonian,* now this writing on your jacket. Has anything else unusual happened to you lately?"

"Not really," he answered, biting down into his hero sandwich.

"What about those phone calls, Paul?" Ned reminded him. He turned to Nancy and explained. "Earlier this week Paul got a few strange phone calls. The caller never spoke—he just listened to Paul say hello and then hung up."

Paul blushed. "Come on, Ned, that was probably just a wrong number."

"Three in one night?" Ned sounded skeptical. "Did you notice anything about the calls?"

Nancy asked sharply. "Did you hear any breathing, or background noise, or static on the line?"

Paul shook his head.

"Then it was probably a local call from a private phone," Nancy concluded.

"Oh, Nancy, you see a mystery in everything," Brook teased, pointing with a french fry. "It must be an occupational hazard for a detective."

Paul looked up. "A detective? Are you a detective, Nancy?"

"She's solved all kinds of cases, Paul," said Brook.

"Do you work with the police or privately?" Paul asked Nancy.

"I just help friends when they get into trouble," Nancy replied, fending off his questions. "Ned, can you pass me the ketchup?" As Nancy dressed up her burger and started eating, she wondered why Paul had seemed so interested in her work. She hated to think badly of him, but something just didn't seem right to her. Was he afraid she'd uncover some secret he was hiding?

After dinner the girls made a brief stop at the Theta Pi house to change into jeans and pick up sweaters. Then the two couples joined the flow of students heading for the football field, where the Dillon Patrick concert was to be held. Night was falling, but old-fashioned lampposts along the curving paths cast pools of warm yellow light.

Ned drew his arm around Nancy, and she slid

her arm under his letter jacket to circle his waist. "Now that you've caught the test thief, we can relax and enjoy the rest of the weekend," he murmured into her ear. She thrilled to the feel of his warm breath ruffling her hair.

The moment with Ned was too nice to spoil with reminders that Carrie Yu may very well not be the thief.

The concert was open to all Emerson students and their guests, as a way of showing off the newly renovated football stadium. By the time Nancy and her friends reached the stadium, the stands were nearly full. "I knew we shouldn't have gone back to change our clothes—now we'll be sitting up in the rafters," Brook groaned.

"I guess we're not the only Dillon Patrick fans," Nancy said dryly.

Glancing around at the stands, she noticed Annie Mercer nearby staring intently at Nancy and her friends. Her bubbly smile and dimples had vanished, leaving her face oddly fierce and cold.

Then Annie turned away, and Nancy felt Ned tug on her hand. Nancy followed her friends up the aisle steps, but she couldn't get Annie's expression out of her mind.

Which of the four of them had she been staring at? Nancy wondered. She'd been friendly to Nancy when they talked earlier that afternoon. Ned didn't know Annie, so he couldn't be the target of her hostility. Annie knew Paul from home, but she'd told Brook she was friends with him—and that wasn't the kind of look you give a friend.

Had Brook antagonized Annie at the Theta Pi party? Nancy asked herself. She'd said the girl had acted strangely, but what had really gone on between them?

"Sorry to disappoint you girls, but we'll need binoculars to see Dillon Patrick from here," Ned joked as they finally spotted four empty seats at the far end of a row high in the stands.

Paul grinned. "Ned and I don't want you two to be distracted by some hunk on stage—we want you to ourselves."

Brook flashed Nancy a happy smile.

To reach their seats, they had to sidle along a narrow steel walkway, past the knees of the other people in the row. They flipped down the plastic seats and settled down, first Paul, then Brook, then Nancy, and finally Ned.

Soon the concert began, with a terrific opening act—a woman rock singer they'd never heard of before. "Dillon Patrick will have to be incredible to top her," Ned declared as they applauded her finale.

"Six months from now, I bet she'll be a hot star. We'll be able to say we saw her first!" Paul agreed.

"Oh, you guys just liked her because she was wearing a leather miniskirt," Brook teased.

The boys took it in good humor. "Well, I'd like

to go get a soda," Ned said. "Can I get anything for anybody else?" As he stood up, his seat flipped up automatically on its steel springs. "Whoa!" He laughed, surprised.

"A lemonade would be great." Brook smiled.

"I'll have a cola," Paul said. He pulled out his wallet, but Ned insisted it was his treat.

"I'll help you carry," Nancy offered, standing gingerly as her seat flipped up.

"We'll stay and save your seats," said Brook.

Paul chuckled. "Now seriously, Brook, who would steal these seats? We're up so high we should be wearing red lights on our heads so that airplanes don't crash into us."

Brook playfully slapped Paul's shoulder, and Ned and Nancy were still laughing as they went back down the row and started down the long flight of open metal steps.

"Brook really brings out the fun side of Paul," Ned commented. "Usually he's so serious he keeps to himself. And he's always trying to save money. I think he misses out on a lot of college life."

"So you really don't know him all that well?" Nancy asked.

"Well, there are other guys I hang out with more," Ned admitted.

At the bottom of the steps was a food stand the Varsity Club had set up for the concert. While Ned bought drinks and popcorn, Nancy looked for a phone to call Carrie Yu again. The closest phone was just outside the stadium fence, and three or four people were lined up waiting to use it. As Nancy stood in line, she idly peered up through the high steel skeleton of the bleachers at the legs and feet of the people sitting way above her.

Finally the phone was free, and Nancy made her call. There was still no answer at Carrie's room, and Nancy hung up the phone, disappointed. Pushing through the milling crowd, she returned to the stadium to find Ned.

She laughed when she finally saw him, struggling to keep four paper cups of soda and two boxes of popcorn upright. "Nan, help!" he gasped.

Nancy deftly lifted the tower of paper cups from him and steadied it with two hands. "What would you do without me, Nickerson?" she teased.

"I was just asking myself the same thing," he replied gallantly.

Carrying the drinks and popcorn, Nancy and Ned trudged back up the steps to their seats. "Wasn't this where we were sitting?" Ned asked uncertainly as they reached their row.

The four seats they'd been sitting in were all flipped up. Both their row and the one in front of it were empty.

"Brook and Paul must have left for a minute," Nancy reasoned. "Maybe they saw someone they wanted to talk to. Let's take their seats so they won't have to step over our knees when they come back."

Ned edged along the walkway in front of the seats, using his knee to flip down his own seat. Following Ned, Nancy needed both hands and her chin to steady the tall stack of cups. Reaching her place, she turned around and sat on her upright seat, flipping it down.

After resting her weight on the seat, Nancy felt herself being tossed forward, tipping at a wild angle.

The drinks in the paper cups fell, splashing over her feet. Slipping on spilled soda, Nancy's right foot shot off into the gap behind the wet metal walkway and the seats in front of her. She slammed into those seats, which flipped down under her weight. She was thrown forward over them in a jackknife.

"Nancy!" Ned cried, dropping the popcorn boxes and reaching down to grab her around the waist. He began to lift her up, but then he slipped on the wet walkway, too—accidentally pushing her down into the gap between the walkway and the next row of seats.

Nancy's right leg, and then her hip and torso, bumped and slid through the opening. Ned desperately grabbed hold of her left leg.

Nancy tipped upside down, dangling under the walkway. Her arms flailed uselessly in empty space.

Chapter

Nine

"HOLD ON, NANCY!" Ned called down to her as he continued to dangle her by her left foot.

"You hold on, too!" Nancy shouted back, trying to keep the fright out of her voice. In the darkness she couldn't see the ground clearly, but the steel girders supporting the bleachers glinted all the way down, and she could tell that it would be a very long drop if she fell.

Feeling her left ankle slip slightly in Ned's grip, Nancy desperately sought a toehold with her right foot. Her toe stabbed against the bottom of the steel walkway and she wedged it into the only crack she could find.

Summoning all her upper-body strength, she raised her shoulders toward the bottom of the bleachers above. With split-second timing, she swung her right arm at the very instant she was closest to the girders. Her fingers slapped against a small steel strut and closed around it.

Tightening her fragile hold, Nancy pulled her body upright. As quickly as possible, she grabbed another strut with her left arm.

Ned took one hand off her ankle and thrust it down through the steel framework. He grasped her left arm firmly. "I'll let your foot go now, Nan," he warned her.

"Okay." Nancy braced herself. As soon as Ned had dropped her leg, he reached down and got a good grip on her other arm.

"Ready?" Ned asked, squatting on the walkway. Nancy nodded. "Okay, then, heave ho!" Ned hoisted her up through the gap between the walkway and the girder behind it.

Nancy twisted her lithe body and squirmed through the space. As soon as her shoulders were above the walkway, she managed to get an elbow up onto the steel plank and pull herself up.

A crowd of students had gathered to watch, unable to help because of the narrow space. As Nancy hauled herself onto the walkway, they let go a collective gasp of relief and then broke out clapping.

Ned sank back onto the walkway, exhausted. Nancy collapsed gratefully into his arms.

"Nancy, Ned, what's going on?" she heard Brook's anxious voice behind the circle of onlookers. Brook pushed her way through the gathering with Paul right behind her.

"Nancy's seat crashed down," Ned reported in a shaky voice. "She fell through the bleachers and almost . . . almost . . ."

Nancy scooped her reddish blond hair away from her perspiring face. "I'm okay, guys," she said calmly. In fact, her heart was still pounding and her muscles were sore, but she flashed her friends a confident smile. "I've had far worse accidents, believe me."

Ned chuckled halfheartedly. "Yeah, but that's only because you get threatened by goons trying to scare you off a case."

Brook's dark eyes grew round. "Do you think that someone was trying to hurt you, Nancy?"

"I doubt it," said Nancy as she got to her feet. She hadn't really considered that angle—but as soon as Brook raised the possibility, her mind started working. Despite her discretion, several people now knew that she was checking into the results of the literature test. Maybe the test thief—whoever he or she might be—had gotten scared and was telling Nancy to cool it!

Just then, the surrounding circle of students broke open to let two campus security officers through. Nancy had worked with various members of the force in the past, but she didn't recognize these two.

"We saw there was some kind of commotion

up here," said the first officer, a middle-aged man with thick glasses.

"Yeah, this girl fell through the stands," said a nearby student.

"Fell through the stands?" the officer said, squinting at Nancy.

"Yes, Officer," Nancy reported. "Luckily, my boyfriend here grabbed my foot in time."

"Well, everything's okay now," the man said. "Why don't you kids go back to your seats and wait for the concert to start."

"Officer?" Nancy stopped him. "The reason I fell was because of my seat." She knelt down beside the flip-up plastic seat and showed them that it had wrenched loose from its steel base.

"I knew those fancy new seats weren't safe," muttered the second officer, a thin, black-haired man with a reddish face. "The way they flip right up when you stand up . . ."

"It had nothing to do with the flipping mechanism," Nancy stated. "See this thick spring here? That's what flips the seat up when you get up. It's a good idea—it keeps the seats folded up when they're not being used.

"But as you can see," Nancy went on, "the spring is intact. It's still attached to the base post. Normally, this metal plate attached to the spring should be bolted onto the seat." Nancy pointed to Ned's seat to show how the seat should have worked. The officers nodded.

"But those bolts weren't attached—and they

weren't broken, either," Nancy finished. "It looks as if somebody may have unscrewed them."

The first officer frowned. Edging Nancy aside, he bent down and peered at the broken seat.

"Maybe they weren't screwed in tight in the first place," the second officer suggested. "The workers only finished the seat renovations a week ago."

Brook shivered. "To think that I was sitting in that seat the whole first act," she said.

"That's right!" Nancy exclaimed. "So it couldn't have been a plan to hurt me. Unless the person forgot where I was sitting. You didn't notice anything wrong with it?" Nancy asked, turning to Brook. Brook shook her head.

"The way that bolt was unscrewed, there's no way you could have sat there without dislodging it," Nancy noted. "I'll bet the damage was done during intermission—after you and Paul got up."

"Did any of you notice anyone tampering with the seat?" the officer asked the students who had been sitting nearby. They shook their heads. "There were lots of people walking around, talking to one another," one guy mentioned.

"This could just have been a prank," the older officer said. "We get a lot of them this early in the year, before you kids have knuckled down to your work."

"It's a pretty dangerous prank," Ned said.

"Well, we'll make our report, and we'll keep an eye out for any other mischief," the officer said. "Meanwhile, why don't you move to other seats and enjoy the music?"

"They sure weren't very helpful," Ned muttered as he and Nancy followed Paul and Brook up the aisle to the last few empty seats.

Nancy shrugged. "What could they do? They can't inspect every seat in the stadium to see if the bolts are loose. And I'm sure they wanted to play down the danger so that other people wouldn't panic." She gingerly tested her new seat with her hand before sitting down.

"You could have been badly hurt, Nancy," Brook said, worried.

"Well, I wasn't," Nancy said. "Thanks to Ned's quick thinking."

"Not to mention my superhuman strength," Ned added, joking. Nancy grinned, then slid her hand warmly into his as they watched Dillon Patrick walk out on stage.

The music was still ringing in Nancy's ears two hours later as she and Ned walked across campus after the concert. Brook and Paul had gone out for a cup of coffee, but Nancy had begged off. After her near-fall from the stands, her muscles were a bit sore, and a good night's rest sounded very appealing.

Ned pulled her against his shoulder as they walked. "Thanks for saving my neck tonight,

Nickerson," she murmured, nuzzling against him, admiring the hard muscle of his shoulder.

"Anytime," Ned replied. "It's the least I can do for you, considering how you've just saved me from being expelled."

"I hope so," Nancy said. "I'll be interested to see what Carrie Yu has to say for herself."

"What *can* she say?" Ned asked. "You've practically caught her red-handed. Why else would she have written those answers on that memo slip?"

"I don't know, Ned," Nancy said. "But remember, you were found with a copy of the answers, too. And you couldn't explain why."

An awkward pause fell between them, and Ned pulled his arm away. "I'd think you'd want to wrap up the case, so I won't get expelled." He sounded hurt, and Nancy cast about in her mind for a tactful reply.

"Of course I don't want you to get expelled," she finally said. "But the dean warned me that I can't give you special treatment. What would it look like if I accused Carrie and then found out she wasn't the thief? I'd rather she confessed to me before I go back to the dean."

"Well, I guess you don't care that my college career is on the line here," Ned said.

Nancy was taken aback. "That's not true, Ned! That isn't true at all! And I *am* working on the case. But it's very—baffling."

"Too baffling for the great Nancy Drew?" Ned asked skeptically, striding ahead.

"No!" she defended herself, walking fast to keep pace. "But all I have is a piece of paper with some letters written on it. I can't prove *when* Carrie wrote them down, or why. And I can't prove that she stole that answer key. She had no more access to it than—"

"Than I did?" Ned snapped back, stopping abruptly. He whirled around, and Nancy could see the cold fire in his dark eyes. "So that's it. You *do* think I'm guilty."

Nancy's mouth dropped open. "What? I've never believed you were guilty, not for a second. But that won't convince Professor Tavakolian—or the dean, apparently. So I've got to catch the *real* thief, to get you off the hook."

"Then you'd better do it pretty fast," Ned said hotly. "I can't get expelled—I love Emerson! I love the basketball team, I love my frat, I love my classes and my friends. I can't believe I'd have to leave, just because I made photocopies for a professor I don't even know!"

Nancy's throat tightened in sympathy. "Please, Ned," she said urgently. "If I'm going to clear your name, I have to do it the right way—not the easy way."

Ned and Nancy locked gazes for a long moment. Then Ned ducked his head and muttered, "Sorry. I guess the pressure is getting to me. Come on, let me walk you back to your house."

At the door of the Theta Pi house, Ned took Nancy in his arms and gave her the kind of hug that made her think that everything was all right. Relieved, she lifted her face to his for a kiss. As they clung together for several minutes, their kiss went well beyond making up. Nancy felt limp in his strong grasp, powerless to do anything other than continue the long embrace. When they finally let each other go, it was slowly, reluctantly.

Her head still spinning, Nancy went inside, hurrying past the girls chatting in the living room. As she passed the small desk in the front hall, the girl sitting there, Mindy Kwong, looked up with a smile. "Hi, Nancy," she said brightly. "Oh, I think there's a message for you." She hunted on the cluttered desktop.

"From Professor Tavakolian?" Nancy asked.

"I don't know—someone just dropped this through the front door mail slot," Mindy explained, holding up a plain white envelope.

Nancy took it and held it close to the desk light, curious to know why it was unmarked. She turned it over and broke open the sealed flap. Inside was a sheet of plain white paper. She unfolded it, discovering a typed note:

Dear Detective, If I were you, I'd check on Paul DiToma. He's the guy who stole that test.

Chapter

Ten

Nancy reread the note in disbelief. Had Paul DiToma stolen the answer key and sold it to Carrie Yu—and maybe to other students as well?

Nancy forced a smile. "Thanks, Mindy. Good night!" She skipped lightly up the front stairs. Mindy was known to be a gossip, and right now Nancy didn't want to supply her with any material.

Alone in the second floor hallway, Nancy studied the mysterious message again. As she thought through the facts, she realized Paul really could have stolen the sheet. He was an English major, so he'd know his way around the English faculty offices. Paul wouldn't have needed to steal the answers for himself, but as Professor Tavakolian had said, other students would pay to get the answers—and Paul was in need of money.

But how did this connect to the mysterious phone calls he'd received, and the ad in the *Emersonian:* "Paul DiToma—I'm waiting for you"?

Could Paul's friendship with Ned somehow be a factor in all this? Nancy felt slightly sick to her stomach at this thought. Ned was very touchy about being a suspect—the last thing she wanted was a reason to doubt him.

One thing was for sure—she'd better get to sleep before Brook came back. How could Nancy talk to Brook, knowing that Paul was under suspicion?

"Oh, Nancy, I can't believe this is all happening," Brook said. She sat up in bed the next morning, hugging her knees to her chest.

Nancy moved around the room, getting dressed. "So you had a good time last night?" she asked, trying to sound noncommittal.

Brook stretched lazily. "We were out until midnight—*it's* the first time I've ever had to use my night key to get in after lockup time!" She giggled. "We just went to the Night Owl diner. But we got talking about everything in the world —our families, classes we're taking, books we've read, places we want to travel to—just everything!"

Nancy buttoned her jeans and pulled her burgundy-colored cotton sweater out of her duffel bag. "So you two really have a lot in common?"

"Oh, it's more than that," Brook said, gushing. "I feel as though I've known him all my life. I can't believe that we only met on Thursday."

As Nancy stepped to the mirror to brush her hair, she felt an ache in her throat. She was glad Brook was happy, but it only made her feel bad that the reason for Brook's happiness was now one of her suspects.

Brook leaned over to check her bedside alarm clock. "Paul and I were going to meet for brunch —do you and Ned want to join us?" she asked.

Nancy slung her purse over her shoulder. "No, thanks—maybe we can double for dinner. Why don't you ask Paul to make plans with Ned?" With a quick wave, Nancy was out the door.

Nancy went downstairs to the phone to call Ned. "I have to track down Carrie Yu this morning," she explained to him. "I'd better do it alone because I need to get her to open up to me."

"Stop by the house when you're done—I'll be waiting to hear what happened," Ned said anxiously. "I'll shoot baskets with Jerry and Rich till you get here. And, Nan—good luck."

"Thanks, Ned," Nancy replied warmly. She hung up and dialed Carrie Yu's number. This time Carrie's roommate answered. She told Nancy that Carrie was taking an orientation tour of the chemistry labs.

Nancy walked across campus to the science labs. The glass front doors were open, and Nancy walked down the empty, echoing corridors. She spotted a few older students in various laboratories—working on long-term projects, she imagined. Otherwise the building was quiet.

Nancy soon found the tour group in progress. A lab director was demonstrating how to use a bank of computer terminals. Nancy spotted Carrie among the students.

Ten minutes later, when the tour was over, Nancy fell into step beside Carrie. "Remember me from Friday?" Nancy asked.

Carrie nodded warily. "You're the English professor's assistant."

Nancy drew a breath. "I'm working for Dean Jarvis as well. We're looking into a possible cheating ring on the literature test."

Carrie stopped still, but she said nothing.

"Look," Nancy went on. "I found this stuck to your shoe." She held up the yellow memo slip, hoping Carrie wouldn't ask how she'd found it.

Carrie stared at the paper, visibly upset.

"These letters match a series of answers on the test," Nancy said. "Did you have these answers stuck on your shoe when you took the test?"

Carrie blinked. "I took them into the auditorium with me," she confessed in a tight voice. "But I didn't use them!"

Hooray! Nancy was thinking—I have my thief.

"How did you get the answer sheet out of the professor's office?" she asked Carrie.

"What office?" Carrie frowned. "A guy stopped me outside the English department office, just after I signed up for the exam. He offered to sell me the test for fifty dollars."

Nancy frowned. "You bought the test?"

"Yes," Carrie said, her eyes cast down in guilt. "Then I took the test to the library and looked up the answers to the questions. I wrote down the letters on three yellow slips—but like I said, I didn't use them!" She looked up pleadingly.

"You got a perfect score," Nancy noted.

"Well," Carrie admitted, "after looking up all that stuff in the library, I—I remembered the right answers without looking."

Nancy reflected for a moment. It was the answer key that had been stolen from Tavakolian's office, not the complete test. Was there another cheating ring at work? Carrie had said a guy sold her the test—that could have been Steve Groff, Gary Carlsen, Tom Mallin, Paul, or even . . . Ned.

"Who sold you the test?" Nancy asked, continuing to grill.

Carrie shrugged. "I don't know his name. He was tall, like an athlete—"

"Dark hair?" Nancy asked, not really wanting an answer.

"Oh, no." Carrie shook her head. "His hair was white blond."

The image clicked in Nancy's mind—Steve Groff.

Fifteen minutes later Ned came charging into the living room of the Omega Chi house, where Nancy was waiting for him. Dressed in baggy sweats, with a basketball under his arm, he was gorgeous, she thought.

Nancy jumped up and flung an arm around Ned's neck, planting an excited kiss on his cheek. "I've got a hot break in the case," she whispered. "Where can we go to talk?"

Ned led her into the empty study lounge, where she quickly recounted her interview with Carrie. "Steve Groff?" Ned whistled. "The same guy who argued with Paul at the party yesterday?"

"It may not just be a coincidence," Nancy said guardedly. Then she showed Ned the note she'd received the night before, accusing Paul of the theft.

"You don't think they're in this together, do you?" Ned asked, aghast.

"I don't know what to think," Nancy admitted.

Ned shook his head. "I can't believe Paul is involved. But you have to talk to Steve Groff."

"I just called his dorm room—he wasn't in," Nancy said.

"You know where he is, most likely," Ned said.

Nancy nodded. "The pool's my next stop."

"Can I come along?" Ned asked. "Steve seems

to be a hothead—you could probably use some backup."

"Sure—thanks."

There were several swimmers doing laps in the big pool when Nancy and Ned arrived. It took them a few minutes to pick out Steve. Watching him churn up and down the pool, Nancy was impressed with his strength and endurance.

As Steve finally emerged, dripping wet, from the pool, Nancy and Ned hurried along the wet tile floor to cut him off. Steve first rubbed his head with a towel, then looked up to see Nancy. He sneered. "I've got nothing more to say to you." When he noticed Ned standing behind her, he hesitated.

"Steve," Nancy said patiently, hoping to keep the encounter calm. "I just talked to Carrie Yu—she said that you sold her a copy of the test."

Steve began to flush. "She bought it!" He protested. "She's as much to blame as I am."

For the moment Nancy let that pass. "We just want to know how you got the copy," she said.

Peering quickly over his shoulder, Steve muttered, "I—I just found it."

"Found it?" Ned repeated in dismay.

"You've got to believe me!" Steve burst out. "I was outside the English department, and I happened to look in a big trash basket in the hall. There it was right at the top. 'Freshman Literature Placement Test.' It was too good an opportunity to pass up! And then that girl walked by and I decided to make a buck. I told her I had the test and asked how much was it worth to her. I made her a photocopy of it for fifty dollars."

"And you don't have any idea how the test got in that trash bin?" Ned asked.

Steve shook his head. "That test could have been stolen by anyone—even Paul DiToma."

Nancy's head jerked back. "Why do you mention Paul DiToma?" she asked quickly.

Steve gave her a sly look. "I ran into him in the department office, just before I found the test copy in the trash."

Nancy recalled Paul saying he'd spoken with Steve in the department office that Monday. Her eyes narrowed. "Did you write me that note about Paul being the thief?"

Steve was too surprised by her deduction to try to lie. "Yeah, I wrote it," he said. "I don't like that guy—so I made that up. But I should have known you wouldn't believe it. He's your buddy. I saw you all together in the student center yesterday."

"That's true," Nancy said. "Was it you who wrote on his leather jacket?"

Steve was obviously confused. "Wrote on what jacket? He wasn't even wearing a jacket when I saw him."

Nancy still was skeptical, but she had no proof

that Steve had been the vandal. "Well, I'll have to tell Dean Jarvis that you took the copy of the test—and that you sold it," she said.

"It was such a stupid thing to do," Steve said. "You know what killed me? I knew most of the answers right off the bat. I would have gotten a good score even if I hadn't found the test. But now they'll never know that."

As Nancy and Ned walked away from the sports complex, they both felt discouraged. "I guess Steve's sorry he cheated now," Ned said. "But that was a rotten thing he did, implicating Paul."

"And he took some trouble to do it—he had to find out where I was staying to leave the note," Nancy added.

"Maybe Steve was hoping to divert you from learning that he'd sold the test to Carrie," Ned said. "He'll get in a lot of trouble for this."

"Unfortunately," Nancy said, "we've caught two cheaters now—Steve and Carrie—but we still don't know who stole the key from the professor's file."

Ned's face darkened. "You mean—I'm not off the hook yet?"

Nancy sighed and shook her head. "Nope. And I don't know how that copy of the test got in the trash bin, where Steve found it."

"I didn't throw a copy away," Ned declared.

"I believe you," Nancy said, "but Professor Tavakolian will probably think you did—after all, you copied the test for him. I'd better not tell the dean what I've learned—not yet."

Seeing Ned's face crease with worry, Nancy hooked her arm in his and gave it a reassuring tug. "I still haven't solved the case," she said gently, "but I'm not giving up yet."

At six-thirty that evening Ned and Paul picked up Nancy and Brook at the Theta Pi house. The four young people headed for a local pizza restaurant. Inside the door, a short line of people waited to be seated, and another line waited for take-out pizzas. Ned waved to a couple of his basketball teammates at a nearby table. Someone in the take-out line behind them said hello to Paul, and he turned around to smile at her. Nancy noticed that it was Annie Mercer.

"Everybody's here tonight," Brook said, gazing out toward the dining room. The brick walled restaurant was dimly lit, with candles stuck in olive oil bottles on each table.

The restaurant owner, a bustling, plump, bald man, handed menus to the kids waiting for tables. "Read these now, and then you'll be ready to order when you sit down," he suggested.

The two couples huddled over the menu. "Let's get one large pizza to share," Ned suggested.

"Great idea," Paul agreed. "I vote for a mushroom pizza."

"Mushroom?" Brook wrinkled her nose.

"Don't tell me you don't like mushrooms!" Paul teased. "And I thought I'd found the perfect girl—well, that's the end of this romance."

Nancy smiled. "We could have half of the pizza with mushrooms, and the other half plain."

"Oh, plain is so boring," Brook said. "How about having spinach on the other half?"

"Spinach? Too healthy for me," Ned joked.

They finally agreed: one-half mushroom, one-quarter spinach, and one-quarter pepperoni. As soon as they were shown to a table, they gave their pizza order to the waiter. Weaving his way through the crowded restaurant, he stuck their order on a spike on the small, high counter leading into the kitchen. He picked up a hot pizza the cook had just set on the counter, sidestepping the owner, who was handing a pizza box to someone in the take-out line.

"The noise level here is unbelievable," Ned shouted across the table.

"What? I couldn't hear." Brook laughed.

Just then a waiter dropped an entire trayful of empty water glasses right next to the counter. The entire restaurant burst into applause. The waiter took a sheepish bow. The other two waiters set down the pizzas they were picking up from the kitchen and helped sweep up the shattered glass.

"I hope the cost of those glasses doesn't come out of his salary." Paul winced. "Last summer I worked in a pizza restaurant, and that's what they did to us if we broke anything."

"After working in a pizza restaurant all summer, aren't you sick of eating it?" Brook asked.

Paul grinned. "Nothing can take away my appetite for pizza. Look, here comes our order."

Their waiter set the hot pizza down in the center of the table. Whipping out a wheeled pizza cutter, he swiftly cut it into eight slices.

"Anyone else want spinach?" Brook asked as she picked up a slice from the spinach portion.

"You know, it does look good." Paul grinned. "I'll give it a try."

Brook laid one of the spinach topped slices on Paul's plate. He picked it up and was about to bite in. "Watch out, it's hot," Nancy cautioned as she tested her own slice.

Paul backed away from the slice and blew on it, dislodging a small clump of spinach. A strange look crossed his face.

"What's wrong, Paul?" Nancy asked.

Paul tilted his slice of pizza toward the candle on their table to study it in the light. Then he laid it down on his plate and poked with his fingers under the mounds of dark green spinach. Nancy leaned over for a better look herself.

Lightly embedded in the cheese, under a clump of spinach, lay a long shard of razor-sharp glass.

Chapter
Eleven

PAUL'S HANDS were shaking as he pushed his plate away. "Suddenly I've lost my appetite for pizza," he said grimly.

"Check the other slices," Nancy ordered Ned and Brook. They inspected the pizza for more pieces of broken glass, but found nothing.

Meanwhile, Nancy craned her neck around, looking for their waiter. The restaurant owner, spotting trouble, hurried to their table. "Can I help you?" he asked.

Paul silently showed him the glass in the pizza slice. The owner grimaced. "That's horrible!" he exclaimed, picking out the glass.

"It's a piece of one of your drinking glasses—it has the same yellow tint," Nancy noted.

The owner seemed perplexed. "Maybe when

the glasses broke, a piece fell into the toppings in the kitchen."

"When the waiter broke those glasses, our pizza was already out of the oven," Nancy informed him. "It was brought to our table right after they finished sweeping up. If you don't mind, could I look around your kitchen?"

The owner hesitated. "They're awfully busy in there. . . ."

"I won't get in the way," she promised. "It'll only take two minutes." She stood up and headed for the kitchen without waiting for an answer. As she'd hoped, the owner didn't stop her.

A doorway to the right of the pass-through counter led into the brightly lit kitchen. One pizza cook stood in a corner, kneading a huge ball of dough. Two others stood at a large marble topped table making the pies.

One pounded some dough into a large flat crust, then spooned on tomato sauce with a metal ladle. The other took handfuls of shredded cheese and sprinkled them over the pie. Then he reached into a bowl of pepperoni slices and scattered them on the top. Watching the pizza makers work, Nancy felt sure they would have noticed a shard of glass when they put toppings on the pie.

When the pies were assembled, Nancy saw the cooks using a wooden paddle to carry them over to a huge iron oven. With the same paddle, they pulled out pizzas that were done and slid them onto round metal trays. Then they tossed the trays onto the counter for the waiters to pick up.

Nancy walked over to the pass-through counter. It ran almost the entire width of the restaurant, ending behind the cashier's desk. The line of people waiting for tables or for take-out snaked along the counter, where hungry customers could be tempted by the smells.

Anyone in the kitchen, or someone from the dining room, could have hidden the piece of glass in their pizza without being noticed, Nancy decided. And the commotion caused by the breaking glasses would have made it all the easier.

Turning for one last look at the kitchen, Nancy saw a familiar figure, standing by the large chrome dishwashing machine. With a canvas apron tied over his jeans and T-shirt, he was obviously the dishwasher. He saw Nancy looking at him and turned away.

It was Tom Mallin!

The restaurant owner bustled up behind Nancy. "Seen enough?" he asked anxiously.

Nancy nodded. "Just one question. How long has Tom Mallin worked here?"

He acted worried. "Two years or more. He's an excellent worker. Why?"

"Just curious." Nancy smiled.

The owner followed her back to her table. "I'm

so sorry your pie was ruined," he said earnestly. "We'll replace it at once."

Ned and Nancy exchanged glances with Paul and Brook. "Uh, thanks," Ned said, "but can we take a rain check? We're not all that hungry anymore."

"Yes, yes, any time you want, you just come back and I'll give you a free dinner," the owner offered. Thanking him, the two couples left.

"We can make it back to the Theta Pi house before they clear away dinner," Brook said, checking her watch. "If anyone's in the mood for heartburn—it's chili night."

"Better heartburn than a sliced-up mouth," Paul said wryly.

"Paul, I'm starting to think someone really has it in for you," Brook declared.

"First the phone calls, then the ad, then your jacket—" Ned added. He stopped himself before he mentioned the note accusing Paul of stealing the test.

"Steve Groff seems to have it in for you," Nancy suggested, gauging Paul's reaction.

Paul seemed puzzled. "But the phone calls and ad were before I met Steve Groff in the English office. He didn't even know my name or where I lived—not until Saturday, when he saw me at the frat open house."

As they walked into the Theta Pi house, Brook ran to pick up the ringing phone on the front desk. "Nancy Drew?" she said. "Why, yes, she's right here." She handed the phone to Nancy.

"Hello?" Nancy said.

"Miss Drew? Frank Tavakolian. I have an interesting bit of news for you. I, er—I have solved our little mystery."

Nancy caught her breath. "You have?"

The professor chuckled sheepishly. "Well, yes. I found the missing sheet of test answers. They were in another file folder in my cabinet. I must have shuffled the papers around when I was putting the files back on Monday afternoon—and I thought I was being so careful. . . ." Nancy could tell that he wasn't the type of man who could easily admit he'd been wrong.

"But, Professor," Nancy said, interrupting him. She spoke in a low voice, so Brook and Paul wouldn't overhear. "There *was* cheating going on. I found two students who got hold of a copy of the test—the whole test, not the answer key."

There was silence at the other end of the line for a moment. Then Professor Tavakolian cleared his throat. "I knew that six perfect scores were too many," he said at last. "So Nickerson *was* guilty—he took an extra copy when he was photocopying, no doubt."

Nancy flushed. "One of the cheaters—Steve Groff—found the test in a trash bin outside the English office, he says, and he sold it to the other student, Carrie Yu. We have no evidence linking Ned Nickerson to the theft." And we never did, she was tempted to add, but she knew it wasn't wise to antagonize the professor.

"But he was the only person besides myself who had access to the test," the professor said huffily. "Perhaps he made extra photocopies to sell."

"He *didn't*—and he swears he didn't throw away a copy of the test," Nancy protested. She tried to keep her voice low because she knew Ned was standing right behind her, listening to every word. "Someone else got hold of it somehow."

"But who—and how?" Tavakolian erupted. "You'd better come up with a culprit soon, or I shall ask the dean to take action against Nickerson!" He hung up abruptly.

After a jog and breakfast with Ned on Monday morning, Nancy took a long, restorative shower in the Theta Pi house. She passed Brook in the hallway. "I'm off to the bookstore—catch you later!" Brook called out with a wave.

Back in the room, Nancy settled down on the bed to make some phone calls. After her last conversation with Professor Tavakolian, she knew more than ever that she'd need concrete evidence to convince him that Ned wasn't guilty.

First she dialed Dean Jarvis to report what she'd learned about Steve Groff and Carrie Yu. Next, she called home. Her father, Carson Drew, was at his law office, but she spoke to Hannah Gruen, the Drews' long-time housekeeper. Nancy explained that she would be staying at Emerson a day or two longer than she'd planned.

Just as she hung up, the phone rang again. It was Ned. "So what's the agenda for today?" he asked.

"Can you come with me to Ivy Hall?" Nancy asked, drying her hair with a towel. "I'd like you to walk me through what happened last Monday."

"At your service," Ned said promptly. "I'll stop by for you in ten minutes, at noon."

Ms. Belzer waved hello as Nancy and Ned walked into the empty department office a half hour later. "If anyone comes in looking for me, I'm going to return these to the library. I'll be back in ten minutes," Ms. Belzer explained, carrying a pile of books out the door. Nancy nodded.

Glancing around, Ned began his story. "Okay. I stopped by Tavakolian's office just after three o'clock. He gave me the test—it was ten pages long. I brought it down here and put the first couple of pages through the photocopier." He moved through the archway into the photocopier nook. "Soon I had to reload the paper tray—two hundred copies use up a lot of paper.

"Then, after I started the copies of page three, I noticed page four was missing," he went on. "So I went back to the professor's office."

Nancy followed Ned back out into the hallway and down to Professor Tavakolian's office, which was locked shut. "You came down here, but he wasn't in," Nancy prompted Ned.

"Right," Ned replied. "I found the disk on his desk and took it back to the department office." They went back up the hallway. "Ms. Belzer let me boot up the disk on her screen," Ned finished, standing before her desk.

"How did you know which file it was?" Nancy asked, trying to visualize the scene.

"There was only one file on the disk, called Frosh Lit Test," Ned recalled. "I scrolled through the file until I found the missing page, then I printed it out."

Nancy thought a minute. "Were the answers in the same file as the test questions?"

Ned nodded. "When I scrolled through the file, I saw the list of answers, at the end of the test questions."

"Okay. Now tell me how you printed out the missing page, step by step," Nancy asked.

Ned explained patiently, "I scrolled through the file to the section that represented the missing page. I highlighted it on screen. Then I hit a series of buttons to tell the printer to print just that page." He pointed to the buttons on Ms. Belzer's keyboard.

Nancy looked around. "You printed it out on this printer on the table by the window?" She paced around the bank of file cabinets over to the window as she spoke.

Ned nodded, following her. "I went to take the

sheet of paper out of the printer. Then I returned to Ms. Belzer's computer, hit the button to exit from the file—"

"You mean you left the computer for a minute, with the test still on the screen?" Nancy asked.

Ned nodded.

"Ned, that may be it!" Nancy said eagerly. She hurried back around the file cabinets and pointed to Ms. Belzer's computer. At the bottom of the screen, the name of the file Ms. Belzer had been working on was clearly displayed: Honors Program.

"Don't you see?" Nancy said eagerly. "The name of Tavakolian's file was Frosh Lit Test. Anyone walking by and glancing at the screen would know at once what this file contained. It was as good as displaying it on TV."

Ned nodded slowly. "But how could anyone have copied down the answers that fast? I was only away from the desk for a minute."

"It wasn't the answers that were stolen," Nancy reminded him, "it was the whole test. Now show me again how you print it out. We'll use Ms. Belzer's file here as an example.

"So with just three keystrokes, someone could have told the computer to print out the whole test," Nancy said after Ned showed her. "That must have been just after you'd left the printer, or you'd have noticed. And then after you'd returned to the computer—the thief went over to the printer and took out the pages." She strolled to the table by the window and lifted out Ms. Belzer's two-page document the laser printer had already printed out.

"Nancy, that's it!" Ned cried.

"And this is a fairly common software program—lots of people must know how to work it," Nancy noted. "Where was Ms. Belzer at the time?"

"She went over to the faculty cubbyholes to put in some mail," Ned recalled. "So someone could have been at the desk without being noticed. There were loads of students roaming around the department office that afternoon—professors, too."

"Anyone specific you can remember?" Nancy kept on. "It'd help us to have other witnesses."

Ned concentrated. "Only one person I remember for sure—Paul DiToma."

Nancy frowned, stowing the pages from the printer in her shoulder bag. "That's right—he said he was here Monday afternoon. That's when he first ran into Steve Groff."

Ned nodded. "Maybe he knows who else was around then. Why don't you ask him? He should be at the Omega Chi house. We can pick up a quick sandwich there."

Ms. Belzer returned, and Ned and Nancy headed back to Greek Row. The campus was beginning to fill up now, and several students called out to Ned as they walked along. It's as though a special glow surrounds Ned, Nancy reflected as she looked up at him. He's one of the top guys on campus. I'm lucky to be with him.

She slid an arm around his waist, and he instantly responded by putting his arm around her shoulder. She turned her head sideways and upward to study his square jaw, generous mouth, and sparkling dark eyes. She noticed his handsome features light up as he saw another friend approach.

He really does love this place, Nancy thought to herself. No wonder he'd be so upset at getting expelled. I have to make sure it doesn't happen!

They parted outside the Theta Pi house, so Nancy could drop off her sweater now that the day was growing hot. She climbed the stairs and walked down the hallway to Brook's room.

The door stood ajar, as usual. The Theta Pi sisters trusted one another so much that they rarely locked or even shut their doors.

As Nancy stepped through the door, a length of rope hanging over the door frame brushed against her head. Surprised, she pulled back.

The rope had been tied in the shape of a noose. Pinned to it was a scrawled note:

Stay away or your going to get hurt!

Chapter

Twelve

NANCY WAS STANDING in the doorway rereading the handwritten note when Brook came up the hall from the bathroom. "Hey, Nancy, where've you been?" she asked cheerfully.

Brook peered over Nancy's shoulder. When she saw the noose, she came to a dead halt. "Whoa," she said softly, clearly shaken.

Nancy tried to slip the note into her pocket, but her jeans were too tight to do it easily. Brook reached out for the paper. "What's that?"

"It came with the noose," Nancy said dryly.

Brook read the note. "What's this all about?"

"Oh, I'm sure it's nothing. It's pretty routine in my line of work."

"But you're not working on a case now," Brook responded, confused.

"Well, maybe just a little case," Nancy admitted. "One of the professors here at Emerson found out that some kids were cheating on a test, and he asked me to look into it. Minor stuff."

"Oh." Brook glanced at the note again. "With this demented handwriting and the lousy grammar, I thought it was from a weirdo or something."

"Nah, it's probably just a nervous student," Nancy guessed, fingering the smooth white sheet of note paper.

"Good." Brook stepped past her into the room. "Because with all this stuff that's been happening to Paul, not to mention your fall at the concert Saturday night, I was starting to worry."

"Well, whatever it is, I'm sure you're in no danger," Nancy reassured her. "But it does mean that I'll need to stay on a couple of days."

"Great!" Brook exclaimed, smiling.

Dropping her sweater on the bed, Nancy said goodbye to Brook, promising to check in with her later. She went downstairs, where Ned was waiting for her, and they walked over to the Omega Chi Epsilon house.

On the way, she showed him the weird note she'd found. Ned frowned, looking worried. "Someone really is trying to scare you off this case."

Nancy shrugged off his concern. "This isn't such a threatening note," she pointed out. "If anything, it tells me I'm closing in on the test thief—and that's good news."

Inside the fraternity house, Ned buzzed Paul's room on the intercom, but there was no answer. "Let's hang out till he shows up," Nancy suggested. "I have a couple more calls I ought to make, anyway. I should check my other suspects' alibis for Monday afternoon, which was probably when the test was printed out from the computer."

"Why don't you use the phone down the hall?" Ned offered. "No one's around." He handed her a copy of the campus directory, and she settled down at the desk.

Her first call was to Tom Mallin.

"Monday afternoon, after three o'clock?" Tom sounded surprised. "I was working at the pizza restaurant."

A quick call to the pizzeria confirmed Tom's alibi. Next, Nancy tried Annie Mercer. She wasn't in, but her roommate Claire promised to have Annie return the call. Nancy phoned Gary Carlsen next.

"He's at the library," his roommate reported.

"But classes haven't even started yet," Nancy replied in surprise.

Gary's roommate gave a sardonic chuckle. "He just likes to browse around there. The other night, in fact, he stayed there all night. He told me he went down into the stacks and hid from the librarians at closing time—nine-thirty. He took a flashlight with him so he could read all night. He says a senior he knows from chess tournaments does it all the time. Bunch of nerds, if you ask me. Want to leave a message?"

"No, thanks," Nancy said, smiling. More than ever, she couldn't imagine Gary being her culprit.

Her last call was to Linda Corrente. "Monday afternoon?" Linda repeated. "A week ago? Let me see—I was in my room, working on a poem."

"Was anybody else there?" Nancy asked.

"No," Linda said. "I need solitude to write."

Not much of an alibi, Nancy thought, but then Linda wasn't a very strong suspect in this case.

"One more question," Nancy said. "Do you use a computer?"

"Not really," Linda answered hesitantly. "I'm taking a crash course on how to use a Mac—they offer it as part of orientation—but I have to say that I'm still pretty lost."

Nancy quickly pictured the English department office's computer. It was an IBM, not a Macintosh. "Thanks. 'Bye." She rang off. Linda clearly didn't know enough about computers to have printed out that test on the spur of the moment.

Just as she hung up the phone, Paul DiToma came strolling out of the kitchen. "Hey, Paul," she called out. "We just buzzed your room—I thought you were out."

"I was in the kitchen. I signed up for lunch dishes duty this week," Paul said. "Now Brook and I are driving out to the country. We'll have dinner at Bob's Barbecue—want to come?"

"No, but can we walk with you to the car?" Nancy asked. Ned grabbed them a couple of sandwiches before they followed Paul out the door.

"I'd like to pick your brain a little," Nancy said.

Paul shrugged. "About what?"

"You remember when I saw you in the English department office last Monday?" Ned asked.

"Yeah, I was picking up a reading list for my modern poetry seminar."

Ned nodded. "Who else was there?"

Paul seemed puzzled, but he slowed to a stop and tried to visualize the scene. "I saw a couple of friends signing up for conferences with their advisers—Larry Bowen and Phil Epstein," he recalled. "Oh, I saw that girl from my hometown, the Mercer twin, signing up for the freshman lit test. And so was Steve Groff. That's when he asked me about Professor McCarty's class and somehow I ticked him off."

"Steve said he found the test in the trash bin right after that," Ned reminded Nancy. "So that really pinpoints the time of the theft."

"What theft?" Paul asked.

"Professor Tavakolian suspected there was some cheating on the placement test for the required literature course," she explained. "Apparently, someone found a copy of the test in the trash bin outside the English department office on Monday afternoon—and sold it to other students so they could cheat."

Paul looked over at Ned. "You were there photocopying the test for Tavakolian, weren't you?" Ned nodded, and Nancy saw Paul putting two and two together. "Tavakolian's accusing *you?*" Paul exclaimed. "That's absurd!"

"Not only that, Paul," Ned declared. "Nancy received a note accusing *you* of stealing the test."

"You've got to be kidding! I'd never steal a test!" Annoyed, Paul began to stride down the sidewalk, and Nancy and Ned scurried to keep up with him.

"Steve Groff admitted to me that he sent the note to make you look bad," Nancy said.

"What does that guy have against me?" Paul complained. "Did he mess up my jacket, too?"

"He says not," Nancy said.

"What about the glass in my pizza?" Paul wondered. "You think that was his handiwork, too?"

Just then they reached the corner where Paul's car, a beat-up black station wagon, was parked. As Paul began to pull his keys out of his pocket, Ned stared aghast at the car. Paul and Nancy followed Ned's gaze. They both stopped suddenly and froze.

The window on the driver's side had been smashed into a mass of small white- and aquatinted crystals. Someone had then jabbed a hole through it.

"No. Not my car, too," Paul moaned softly.

He reached in through the hole and popped up the door lock. As he opened the door, Nancy glimpsed a piece of paper on the seat.

"Can I look at that note, Paul?" Nancy asked him in a level voice.

Paul nodded dumbly, picked up the paper, and handed it to Nancy. He and Ned read it over her shoulder:

You think your really cool but, I'm telling you now, you cant get rid of me this way. Your going to pay for this!

Chapter

Thirteen

THE NOTE WAS handwritten on a plain white piece of paper. Nancy recognized the writing at once. It was the same as the handwriting on the note attached to the noose in Brook's room that morning!

"I knew I shouldn't park my car on the street," Paul muttered.

Nancy turned to look him straight in the eye. "Paul, you've got to face up to the fact that *somebody*—either Steve Groff or someone else —really has it in for you," she said firmly. "And that person is connected to this stolen test. I'll explain the connection in a minute, but first, we have to call the police."

"The police?" Paul fretted as Nancy began to walk toward the phone booth across the street.

"This isn't just vandalism," Nancy explained

as he followed her. "The note that was left on the seat is pretty threatening. Who knows how far this person will go?"

When the police operator answered, Nancy asked for Sergeant Weinberg, the police officer she'd worked with on previous cases. She briefly explained to Weinberg what had happened to Paul's car, and he agreed to come and investigate right away.

Paul and Nancy waited on a grassy bank by Paul's car. Meanwhile, Ned took off to pick up Brook. Soon they returned, with Brook wearing a hot-pink T-shirt and khaki pants. Paul showed Brook the note found in his car.

"It's the same handwriting as the note on that noose, Nancy!" Brook declared.

Nancy nodded, fishing her note out of the pocket of her jeans to compare with Paul's.

"Nancy, you said Steve Groff confessed that he sent you that other note—the one about me," Paul mused, idly plucking blades of grass. "Do you think he wrote these two notes, too?"

"It may just be a coincidence," Nancy answered cautiously. "His note was typed, and these two are handwritten."

"Did his note have the same bad spelling?" Brook asked.

Paul managed a little smile. "You can tell she's an English major," he kidded.

"That's a good point, Brook," Nancy said. "I'll have to inspect the three notes carefully."

When Sergeant Weinberg arrived, however, he took the note from Steve's car and began to put it into an evidence bag. "Sergeant," Nancy said. He stopped and looked at her questioningly. "That note could be a very useful clue in this case I'm working on now."

"But I have to include this in my report," the sergeant said. "Can I photocopy it for you?"

She looked doubtful. "I need to examine the paper type, to compare it to some other notes I've received lately. They all may be connected."

The sergeant was interested. "If they're connected, I should see all of them myself."

Nancy felt frustrated. "I'll make you a deal, Sergeant," she said. "I'll bring what I have down to the station house, and we can go over all of it together."

"Done," the police officer said with a grin.

While the sergeant checked out Paul's car, Nancy ran back to the Theta Pi house to collect her evidence. Ned and Brook went back to their houses to wait while the sergeant drove Paul and Nancy to the station.

Paul filed his end of the report as Sergeant Weinberg led Nancy to a small interrogation room. It was furnished with a steel table, three sturdy wooden chairs, and a strong desk lamp. Nancy spread out the various documents she had gathered on the table and took out her magnifying glass from her purse.

The sergeant disappeared for a moment and

came back with a light table—a large, flat metal box with a glass window on the top. An electric bulb inside lit up the window, making it possible to inspect the documents carefully.

Nancy explained to the sergeant the facts of her case, then placed the three notes on the light table. As she and Brook had noticed, the two handwritten notes—the one with the noose and the one from the car—were clearly written in the same handwriting. The stationery was the same, too, an 8-by-11 sheet of smooth white rag paper.

The typed note from Steve Groff, however—the one that accused Paul of stealing the test—was on a cheaper paper. Nancy noticed at the edge of the sheet a few shreds of dried yellow adhesive, as if it had been pulled from a pad.

"We know that Steve Groff sent this," Nancy told the sergeant, pointing to the typed note.

"The two handwritten notes are clearly from one person—but probably not this Steve Groff," Weinberg said thoughtfully, poring over the notes.

Nancy bit her lip. "Why not? I'd like to see a sample of his handwriting, at least, before I rule him out."

Next she placed on the light table the copy of the test answers Ned had found in his geology textbook. "This looks just like the answer key that was originally stolen," she told Weinberg. "It was placed in Ned's textbook, I assume to frame him for stealing the literature test."

"But I thought you said the answer key wasn't stolen after all," Weinberg said, in some confusion.

Nancy nodded. "The *professor's* answer key was found later—but I think another answer key *was* stolen, straight off the computer, along with the rest of the test. And it must have been printed out on the English department computer."

Next to the answer key, she placed the two-page document she and Ned had printed out in the English department that morning. "This is from that printer—same paper, same typeface."

Weinberg absentmindedly pulled at his earlobe as he thought. "So you think the person who printed out that test kept only the answers and threw the rest of the test away?"

"Yes—and Steve Groff conveniently found it." Nancy finished his thought. "It seems pretty stupid to throw away the test, though."

"Maybe he or she thought it would be easier to carry just one sheet of paper out of the building," Weinberg speculated. "Besides, once someone had the answers, who'd need the test?"

Studying the documents, Nancy frowned. "The typeface on Steve Groff's note is entirely different from the English department's laser printer," she pointed out. "The letters on Steve's note don't have serifs—those little crosspieces on the ends of letters."

"So he used his own computer for that note," Weinberg said. "That doesn't prove he didn't use the English department's computer last Monday."

Nancy sighed. "Right. You see how complicated this case is?"

The police detective nodded thoughtfully, looking from one document to another. "Let's assume that the person who planted this test to frame Ned was the same one who left threats for you and for Paul DiToma."

"I can see why the person who framed Ned would want to scare me off the case," Nancy agreed. "Both actions were designed to disrupt my investigation. But why would that same person want to harass Paul DiToma?"

"This note says he stole the test," Weinberg said, pointing to Steve Groff's note.

"No, Steve Groff just made that up," Nancy explained.

Weinberg groaned. "At least you've got a handwriting sample to go on."

"That's true," Nancy said, considering it. "Maybe that should be my next move—to check all of my suspects' handwriting. Thanks, Sergeant!"

In the main room of the station house, Paul had finished filing his report. Sergeant Weinberg asked a patrol officer to take Paul and Nancy back to campus.

"You can drop me off at the administration building," Nancy told the officer as they reached the college.

"But, Nancy, it's almost six o'clock," Paul said. "Why don't you call it a day? I know Brook and I won't be going anyplace tonight."

"Just one thing I have to check," Nancy replied. "Tell Ned I'll call him in a half hour or so." She hopped out of the car and ran up the front steps of the administration building.

Ms. Karsten was still at her desk in the admissions office, though most of the staff had left. She looked surprised to see Nancy poke her head through the office door.

"I'm glad I caught you," Nancy said. "Can I take another look at the freshmen files?"

Ms. Karsten looked at her watch. "I'm leaving in five minutes."

"Oh, you don't have to see me out," Nancy assured her. "I'll pull the door shut after me."

The admissions director was hesitant, but she finally agreed.

Seated once again beside the huge files, Nancy went directly to the second drawer and pulled out Steve Groff's folder. On his application form, she found several paragraphs of his handwriting—a cramped, angular hand. It wasn't at all like the writing on the noose note and the note from Paul's car. "So we know Steve isn't our culprit," Nancy muttered to herself.

Who next? Nancy remembered that Paul had said that Annie Mercer was in the English department office at the same time he was. Annie wasn't a strong suspect for stealing the test—her grades were too good. But Nancy decided to check her handwriting anyway.

Thumbing through Annie Mercer's file, Nancy could find no handwriting. Everything, from her application form to her correspondence, had been typed, using a fairly common serif typeface.

Then as Nancy riffled through the file a second time, a letter caught her attention. She pulled it from the file and read it curiously:

March 4
Dear Admissions Director:
I am glad to accept your offer of a place in the freshman class at Emerson. Just one thing I thought you should know. I like to go by my middle name, Ann. All my friends call me Annie. So from now on, please address all correspondence to me as Annie Mercer, not Rona Mercer.

See you in the fall!

Sincerely,
Annie Mercer

Nancy felt a prickle running up her neck. She knew that feeling—it meant she was just about to solve a case.

She flipped the file folder shut and looked at the name tab. It read: Mercer, Rona Annie.

Nancy knew that Annie Mercer had a twin sister—named Rona. That meant that all of the application material had been filled out by Rona, not Annie. And somehow Annie was now passing herself off as her twin sister.

That meant that Annie Mercer might not be such a hotshot student after all.

That meant that she very well might have needed to steal that literature test!

Chapter

Fourteen

Nancy ran out of the admissions office, automatically locking the door as she pulled it shut behind her. Her mind was racing as she strode out of the building.

Why would Annie use her sister's application to get into college? The obvious reason would be that her own grades weren't good enough, Nancy reasoned. But she'd have a hard time keeping up academically after she'd started college.

So that gave her a motive for stealing the literature test. Not only that, but Annie had been at the English department office at the right time—Paul had seen her there.

Paul! Nancy's mind clicked even faster. Annie knew Paul from their hometown. Besides Steve Groff, she was the only one of the freshman suspects who also knew Paul DiToma.

Why would she harass him, though? She'd told Brook she was a friend of Paul. Though, as Nancy recalled, Paul said he didn't know her very well.

In the twilight Nancy hurried over to Annie's dorm. She hoped Annie wasn't in now because Nancy needed to find some concrete evidence before she could accuse Annie of stealing the test or harassing Paul.

Nancy took the stairs two at a time up to Annie's room. Pausing before the door, she caught her breath, then knocked.

A voice called from inside, "Come in!"

Nancy turned the doorknob and stepped into the room. Annie's roommate, Claire, sat on the bed, cradling the phone against her shoulder. "Oh, sorry to bother you," Nancy apologized. "I'm Nancy Drew—I called Annie earlier today."

As she spoke, she sidled farther into the room toward Annie's bed. She could see Annie's yellow spiral notebook lying right on the pillow. If she could get that, she'd have a sample of Annie's writing. Claire rolled her eyes. "Still trying to borrow that book? Hang on." She turned away to speak into the phone. "Can I call you back?"

While Claire was murmuring sweet goodbyes, most likely to her boyfriend, Nancy moved to the bed. Facing Claire, she stood in front of the notebook. With one hand, she deftly reached behind herself, grabbed the notebook, and slipped it up under the back of her baggy navy sweater.

Claire hung up the phone. "Annie's down in the dining hall. What book was it you wanted?"

"Oh, I'll just pop down there and find her, okay?" Nancy said brightly. "Sorry to bother you." In a flash, she backed out of the room.

Once the door was closed behind her, Nancy took Annie's notebook out of her sweater and clutched it fiercely. She flew down the stairs to the lobby and glanced around nervously. Straight ahead, she could hear a roar of conversation through the doors of the dining hall. Annie was in there—Nancy mustn't let her see her.

An archway to her right led to another set of stairs, descending to the basement. Nancy dashed down the stairs.

In the basement hallway, two doors stood on either side; on one was printed LAUNDRY ROOM and on the other STUDY LOUNGE. Remembering how deserted the Omega Chi's study lounge was these days, Nancy decided to slip in there.

The lounge was a long, carpeted room with several armchairs and low tables scattered around. Nancy pulled two armchairs together, then snuggled down onto the carpet behind them. If anyone came into the room, they wouldn't see her right away.

Nancy opened Annie's notebook to the first page. It was the beginning of a journal:

Sunday

Its so cool here at college! The campus is really neat, and my roomate Claire seems really sweet. I just know we are going to be best friends!

The handwriting was large and sloppy, with letters tilting every which way. It looked like the same writing as the two notes, though she'd have to inspect them side by side to be sure.

Before she shut the notebook, she had a sudden thought. Maybe Annie had written in her journal about stealing the test! Nancy couldn't resist the temptation to read on.

My dorm is only a few minutes from Greek Row, I went over there today to see where Paul lives. The Oh Mega Ki house looks like an old castle. I looked for his car but I coun't see it. So when I got back to the dorm I called him. It was so nice to hear his voice again! I just know that things are really going to happen between us now that we are both at Emerson together. It was hard the last two years seeing him only when he came home from school, but I think he really cares for me. Ever since that party at Ryan Kellys when Paul sat and talked with me, I know theres chemistry between us. Now I won't have to just wait until I run into him at the

mall or at Dairy Maid, I can see him every
day!

So Annie had a crush on Paul! Well, Nancy
thought, I can't blame her. But Paul had said he
didn't even know that Annie was on campus
until Monday. If she had called him on Sunday,
she must have suddenly felt nervous and not
spoken to him after he answered. She could have
been his mysterious caller!

Hidden behind her chairs, Nancy read on. She
lost all sense of her surroundings as she followed
Annie's private thoughts. On every page some
new piece of the puzzle fell together.

Talked to Rona on the phone tonight, she
says she really likes Yale. She said how funny
it was she never knew I was even applying to
Emerson, Woun't she laugh if she knew I
used her grades to get in!

My adviser is such a jerk! I told her I din't
want to take those tests to get out of courses,
but she said "with my record it shoud be a
snap." Well at least I have the literashure
one covered, I was lucky and saw that guy
typing it up on the computer. Now if I can
just hide the answer sheet good when I go
into the test Ill be fine.

I wonder if Paul saw the ad. He just has to

know its from me! I wonder why he has'nt called yet.

I bet that girl who called and wanted to talk to me about the test knows I stole the answers. But I took care of that. This afternoon I saw that cute guy who was typing the test on Monday—he was in the bookstore talking to Paul! I still had my copy of the answers in my notebook, so I waited till he layed his books down and stuck it inside. Now hes the one wholl get in troubel. Hah!

At first, Nancy felt sorry for Annie as she read her deluded version of events. But as she went on, Annie sounded more and more disturbed.

There all in this together! that nosy Nancy girl, her dumb jock boyfriend, and that redhead witch from Thada Pie. Like they dont want Paul to see me any more. But I fixed Brook good, I messed up her skaggy leather jacket—that *thief* who steals boyfriends!

I guess I din't take out the right screws from Brooks seat, I saw her after the concert and she was'nt hurt—too bad!

Paul was at the pizza place with her again! He cant really like her, she was so snotty about mushrooms on the pizza. I love mushrooms, Paul! Well, maybe she wont like spinach pizza so much after the surprise I stuck in it for her. I hope it slashed her mouth up so good, shell never be able to kiss again.

I wonder if that witch Brook screamed when she found the little present I left in her room! If I coud only get a real rope around her stuck-up neck! Then maybe Paul woud understand that Im the only girl for him!

Nancy laid down the notebook, dumbstruck So it was Brook whom Annie was harassing all the time! It was just coincidence that other people—namely Paul and Nancy—were hit instead.

Leafing to the last page, Nancy read on.

I hope Paul was'nt mad about what I did to his car, I din't want to break the window, but I got so mad when I saw him still with that witch. Theres only so much I can take. But I dont want to hurt him—hes my true love. Shes the one who has to pay. Im not going to let her off easy anymore, I have a plan that will fix her for good!

How far would Annie go? Nancy wondered anxiously. This last entry sounded awfully deranged. Had the pressures of so much deception finally made Annie crack?

Nancy slipped the notebook under her sweater again and hurried from the study lounge. She'd have to call Dean Jarvis—maybe he could get Annie some help before she did something awful. But first she'd have to find Brook to warn her.

Nancy jogged back to the Theta Pi house. As she came in the front door, a bunch of girls were sitting in the living room. "Hey, Nancy!" called out Kristin Seidel. "Come on in and join us!"

"Uh, no thanks. Have you seen Brook?" Nancy asked.

"No," Kristin and the others called back.

Nancy ran up to Brook's room. It was dark. Hoping Brook would be back soon, she switched on the light. Then Nancy reached for the phone to call Ned. She felt guilty for not having been in touch earlier. It was past nine o'clock and she'd said she would call him in a half hour at six.

She groaned when she got a busy signal. Though the red light on Brook's answering machine wasn't blinking, Nancy punched the message button to replay the most recent messages. Maybe Ned had called looking for her, she thought.

The tape on the machine began to play. A bubbly, bright voice filled the room.

"Hi, Brook, this is Annie Mercer. I met you at the Theta Pi open house? Remember how you said you'd love to see my high school yearbooks, to see pictures of Paul? Well, I have them with me now. Could we meet at the entrance to the library at nine-twenty tonight?

"Don't be late, the library closes at nine-thirty tonight," Annie added.

With fear stabbing at her heart, Nancy looked down at her watch. It was nine-fifteen now.

She had to get to the library at once. Who knew what Annie's jealousy would lead her to do to Brook.

Chapter

Fifteen

Nancy paused only long enough to call Ned again. This time he answered. "Nancy, where have you been?" he asked as he heard her voice. "Paul said you'd call me at six-thirty."

"There's no time to tell you the whole story," Nancy replied. "But Annie Mercer is our culprit —she stole the test *and* she's been harassing Paul. Only it isn't Paul she's after, it's Brook. Now she's got Brook alone at the library, and I'm afraid she'll do something awful to her!"

"How can I help?" Ned asked quickly. After knowing Nancy for so long, he was used to leaping into action.

"Call campus security and tell them to meet you at the library," Nancy ordered. "And call Dean Jarvis—tell him we've got a very disturbed student on our hands. Then you go wait outside the front entrance, and don't let Annie escape."

"You've got it," Ned said.

Nancy hung up and raced out the door.

The library was all the way across campus. Sprinting, Nancy felt her lungs burning by the time she made it to the entrance. Two lampposts lit up the small paved area in front of the library. A few low shrubs flanked the two steps leading up to the glass doors.

Looking around as she gasped for breath, Nancy saw no sign of Annie or Brook. And there was no one else around, either.

"Let's hope Brook was smart enough not to come," Nancy muttered. But she had a feeling that Brook, blinded by her infatuation with Paul, would have fallen for Annie's ruse.

Nancy pulled open the glass door and went in. Just inside the entrance was a small carpeted vestibule, with three turnstiles blocking the way to the main reading room beyond.

A bored-looking guard sat yawning on a chair by the turnstiles. As Nancy began to charge through, the guard looked up. "Library's about to close," she drawled.

Nancy wheeled around, frustrated. "It's an emergency," she panted.

"Can I see your ID?" the guard asked.

"I'm not an Emerson student," Nancy protested, "but please—someone may be in danger!

137

Call Dean Jarvis—he'll vouch for me." She gave the guard the dean's home number. "It's okay to call him at home," she urged when the guard acted reluctant to help.

The guard picked up a black phone, dialed a number, and waited briefly.

She looked apologetically at Nancy. "The line's busy," she reported.

It must be Ned on the phone with the dean, Nancy thought, groaning inwardly. "Please try again!" she begged. "He'll be off in a minute."

The guard nodded and patiently dialed again. This time, there was an answer. "Dean, this is Imelda at the library," she said. "I've got a girl here—" She looked up at Nancy. "What did you say your name was?"

"Nancy Drew!"

"Nancy Drew," the guard repeated. "And she says— What? . . . Oh, yes, sir. Thanks." The guard stared at Nancy with sudden respect as she hung up the phone. "He says you can go anywhere you want."

"Thanks!" Nancy pivoted and raced on into the main reading room, which had high ceilings and was brightly lit. Bookcases ran around all four sides, while the room's interior was occupied by two rows of long tables, hard-backed chairs, and a few clusters of upholstered chairs. Only a few students sat around, and they were packing up to leave. With one careful sweep of her eyes, Nancy could tell that Brook and Annie weren't there.

She sprinted into a small side room, lined with rows and rows of wooden drawers, which held an immense card catalog. No one was there.

Tiny prickles of fear ran up Nancy's spine—she was beginning to feel desperate. Running to the far side of the reading room, past the long checkout desk, she noticed another room that was full of magazines and newspapers. No one was in there, either.

Nancy stood in the doorway, willing herself to calm down and think clearly. The library was a big building—she'd never find them if she darted around at random. Maybe, if she thought, she could figure out where they would be.

Then it came to her—the stacks! They were completely hidden from sight, an ideal place for a person crazed with revenge to take a victim. But there were several floors of stacks. Which level would they be on?

The entrance to the stacks was a small open doorway next to the checkout desk. Nancy jogged over there and studied a small floor plan posted by the doorway.

Ned's carrel, she knew, was on the third level, with the political science books. But Brook was an English major. If she had a carrel, it would be with the English books. Nancy studied the floor plan. It told her that the English books were down on the first level, deep underground.

Just beyond the doorway, a metal spiral staircase led down into the stacks, twisting like a corkscrew into the depths. Nancy headed for the stairs. Holding on to the central post with one hand, she swung down the spiral, going as fast as she could on the narrow metal steps.

She was dizzy by the time she reached the bottom level. It was dimly lit, with only a few bulbs along the long central aisle. Nancy peered down the seemingly endless rows of bookshelves. She couldn't see anybody, but she had a sense that someone was there.

Nancy moved as quietly as she could, glad that she happened to be wearing her rubber-soled cross-trainer shoes. With all her senses on alert, she went toward the far end of the aisle.

Then a tiny scuffling sound to her left caught her attention. Nancy turned and caught a glimpse of hot pink—the color of the T-shirt Brook had been wearing earlier.

Just then an electric bell began to chime for closing time. Nancy heard hard-soled shoes clanking down the metal steps. She ducked into a narrow space left between two of the sliding bookcases on their long tracks. If the librarians alerted Annie to her presence, she feared that Annie might get spooked and hurt Brook.

The faint scuffling at the far end of the bookcases stopped, too.

A librarian strode briskly down the aisle, then headed back toward the stairs. As she reached the spiral stairs again, Nancy heard her flick a switch.

The stacks were plunged into darkness.

Nancy groped her way toward the section of bookshelves where she'd seen Brook's shirt. As she got closer, she heard muffled grunting and thrashing about.

Digging into her purse, Nancy pulled out her pocket flashlight. Stealthily, she squeezed around the far end of the bookshelves, into a back aisle lined with carrels.

Now she heard more distinct grunts and a sharp bang as someone knocked against a nearby carrel's steel partition. Judging the direction carefully, Nancy snapped on her flashlight.

The light caught two struggling figures. As they froze in the sudden glare, Nancy could see Annie, clutching Brook's head with one hand. With the other hand, she held a sharp paring knife at Brook's throat!

Nancy flashed her light in Annie's face, momentarily blinding her. She spoke in a low, firm voice. "Annie, let her go."

Annie only stiffened and tightened her grip on Brook. "No!" she snarled. "She stole my boyfriend. Now I'm going to make sure she never steals another boy again."

Brook yanked her mouth away from Annie's smothering hand. "What are you talking about?" Brook burst out. "You were never dating Paul. He barely knows who you are!"

Annie's eyes glittered feverishly in response to Brook's words. Nancy gestured to Brook to remain quiet.

"Annie, what did you have in mind?" Nancy asked, still in a calm, low voice.

Annie pressed her arm across Brook's windpipe and pushed the knife up under Brook's chin. "I'm going to slice up her face, so that no guy will ever be interested in her again," she replied without pity.

Just then, loud voices and pounding footsteps were heard from the next level up. "Annie, they're coming for us," Nancy said, hoping she was speaking the truth. "I asked Ned to bring in the campus police if I didn't meet him outside at nine-thirty. The game is up—let her go."

Annie hesitated for a moment. Momentarily gathering her strength, Brook knocked Annie's knife hand away and dove into the narrow aisle between a nearby pair of bookshelves.

As the footsteps came clattering down the metal steps, Annie whirled around and moved suddenly out of sight. Nancy heard her dodge into another space between some shelves, a few rows farther along.

Nancy turned and shone her light into the aisle where Brook lay, dazed and shaken. "Come on, let's get out of here," Nancy urged Brook. She scurried into the aisle and knelt down to pull her friend to her feet.

But just then, the two girls heard a nearby

creak of metal wheels. Annie was cranking the heavy bookshelves along the tracks, moving the shelves toward them.

Rolling along, the steel shelves were quickly picking up momentum. In a moment's time they would crush Nancy and Brook!

Chapter

Sixteen

THERE WASN'T TIME to get out of the way. As the heavy bookshelf began to roll toward them, Nancy scrambled up from her knees. She wedged her hips against the shelves in back of her. Her weight was pushing them slowly backward.

Groping for the approaching shelf with both hands, Nancy straightened her arms and braced herself. In an instant her shoulders were slammed back against the shelves behind her, but she kept her arms locked and straight.

By now, Brook had recovered somewhat and was staggering to her feet. She shoved her shoulder against the moving shelf, jamming a foot against the shelves behind her. In the darkness the two girls strained to keep a space open between the heavy rolling shelves.

Just then, the searchers coming down the stairs

found the light switch. The dim lights snapped back on. "Nan, where are you?" she heard Ned call out.

"Over here!" Brook shouted.

"Left side!" Nancy added.

The shelf behind the girls jolted to a stop. The bookshelves had rolled until there were no open spaces left in that direction. Now it was only Nancy and Brook's combined strength that kept the shelf in front of them from squashing them.

The searchers were still far down the aisle, but their footsteps pounded closer.

Then the shelf the girls were pushing against was suddenly released. Nancy and Brook tumbled to the floor as the shelves swung away from them.

Nancy looked up just in time to see Annie dash along the side aisle, heading for the exit.

Nancy leapt to her feet and chased Annie. "Ned, block the stairs!" Nancy called out.

"Got it!" she heard Ned call from the center aisle, while footsteps hammered back toward the stairs.

Though the side aisle was almost dark, Nancy could see Annie's figure at the end. Annie swung around the far corner, out of sight.

Then Nancy heard Annie's sneakers squeak to a stop on the linoleum floor. Annie's voice cried out, "Paul!"

Racing around the corner of the shelves, Nancy saw Annie facing Paul DiToma. The knife still gleaming in her grasp, she swayed warily from side to side, as though she might spring at any minute.

"Calm down, Annie," Paul said in a soft, soothing voice. "Drop the knife. Everything's going to be okay now."

Annie's shoulders heaved with emotion. "How could you possibly love Brook instead of me?" she cried. "I've been true to you for almost two years now. She'll never love you the way I do."

Peering over Annie's head, Paul gave Nancy a perplexed, shocked look. But he didn't lose his cool. "Why, I haven't really had a chance to get to know you yet, Annie," he said gently. He held out a hand. "If you'll just give me that knife, maybe we can go have some tea at the student center. It'd be nice to sit and talk awhile."

Annie stood still for a long moment, staring at Paul. Then, with a sob, she dropped the knife onto the floor.

Paul stepped forward and put his arm around Annie. She collapsed, weeping, against his chest. He led her gently toward the stairs.

Nancy scooped up the knife from the floor, then followed Annie and Paul to the center aisle.

All the way down the aisle, Nancy saw Ned standing with a protective arm around Brook. A pair of campus security officers waited beside them. They all seemed to understand that, for the moment, Annie was best left alone with Paul.

Paul went up the spiral stairs first, drawing

146

Annie gently by the hand after him. "Do you remember that night at Ryan Kelly's party?" she asked him in a wistful voice.

"Uh, sure I do," Paul answered softly. "But why don't you refresh my memory?"

"I was sitting on the sofa," Annie recalled dreamily. "And you came over and asked me what kind of dip was on the table, by the corn chips. And I said it was salsa, and you said . . ." Her voice grew faint as they climbed upstairs.

One of the security officers pulled out his walkie-talkie and radioed to two more officers posted outside. "A boy will be bringing the perpetrator outdoors in a minute," he alerted his fellow officers. "He seems to have her under control. Can you take them to the infirmary?"

"Will do," the officer outside radioed back.

"Dr. Singh is waiting at the infirmary," the officer explained to Nancy, Brook, and Ned. "He'll keep her there overnight for observation. Why don't you three head on back to your rooms?"

"Gladly," Ned said. "I think we could all use a good night's rest."

"I really owe you an apology," Professor Tavakolian said to Ned the next morning in Dean Jarvis's office. "I was so certain my answer key had been stolen, I guess I needed a scapegoat."

"Well, if you hadn't filed that answer key in the wrong drawer, we would never have asked Nancy to investigate this case," Dean Jarvis pointed out. "And then we wouldn't have learned that Annie Mercer needed help."

"I'm just sorry I didn't discover her story earlier," Nancy said. "Brook could have been seriously hurt by any of Annie's acts."

"Well, Annie will be leaving Emerson now," the dean explained. "Her parents have come to take her home, where she'll get the psychiatric help she needs. Maybe in a year or two she'll be ready to try college again, though I don't think she'll want to return to Emerson."

"Even if she could get in, with her grade average," Ned added.

The dean shook his head. "She wanted so much to be smart—like her twin sister. And she wanted to go to Emerson so badly, she took a shortcut to make sure she'd get in. Apparently she'd begun to lose touch with reality a long time before she arrived on campus."

"By the way, Dean, what happened with Steve Groff and Carrie Yu?" Nancy asked.

"Steve and Carrie have been placed on academic probation," Dean Jarvis reported. "And Steve has also been suspended from the swim team for a year. But I didn't expel them—they're both basically good kids. They just couldn't resist the temptation of an easy high grade. Getting a good score became more important to them than learning. I guess this incident shows all of us that we need to downplay academic competition—some students can really crack under the pressure."

"I'm throwing out the results of the multiple-choice section of the test," Professor Tavakolian said. "Students will be judged solely on the basis of the essay questions, which I finished scoring this morning."

"And what were the results?" Nancy asked him.

"No surprises," the professor said, smiling. "Linda Corrente and Gary Carlsen both got top scores. Tom Mallin's was not quite good enough to place out of the literature course. After all, he tried to learn about literature by cramming for a few days—he didn't really read all the books, like Linda and Gary did. You can't force-feed that kind of knowledge."

"So Tom, Carrie, and Steve will have to take the required literature course after all," Dean Jarvis said. "That's not so horrible."

"Actually, I remember that that class was kind of fun," Ned declared.

"You, Ned?" Nancy teased him. "Calling an English class fun?"

Laughing, the dean shook Nancy's and Ned's hands and showed them to his office door. As they walked out, Nancy saw a middle-aged couple on the bench outside. Next to them sat Annie Mercer.

Nancy met Annie's eyes, but the blond girl didn't even seem to recognize her. She's really snapped, Nancy thought, with a shiver.

Then the girl turned to her mother. "When will they let us see Annie, Mom?" she asked.

"After we talk to the dean, we can pick her up at the infirmary, Rona," Mrs. Mercer replied.

So the girl on the bench *wasn't* Annie—it was her twin sister. Nancy walked on, feeling goose bumps prickle on her skin. It was uncanny how much the two of them looked alike.

Ned walked Nancy back to the Omega Chi Epsilon house. Her blue Mustang was parked by the curb outside, ready for the drive home. Brook sat on the hood, and Paul leaned against the fender.

"There's only one thing that bothers me about your solving this case, Drew," Ned said as he and she walked up to her car.

"What's that, Nickerson?" she asked.

"It means that you'll be leaving Emerson." He gave her nose a playful poke.

"But you know, Nan," said Brook, "there's always room for you at Theta Pi. That is, if you ever have any reason to come back to visit."

"Oh, I just might find a reason." Nancy smiled meaningfully at Ned.

"Well, I'm glad I got a chance to meet you, Nancy," Paul said, reaching out to shake her hand. "I have you to thank for introducing me to

Brook—and for keeping Brook from being hurt by Annie."

"What else are friends for?" Nancy replied. Then she turned to Brook and gave her a big hug.

"Me next," Ned interrupted. Nancy turned to Ned and slipped into his comforting arms. "You know I hate mushy goodbye scenes," he said lightly. "So let's just say, 'See you later.'"

"See you later," Nancy echoed. He brushed her forehead with a kiss and let her go. With one last wave, she climbed into her car, switched on the motor, and pulled away.

Nancy was fine until she reached the edge of campus. Then her eyes welled up with tears. Brushing them impatiently away, she tried to concentrate on her driving.

But just as she turned onto the highway that led to River Heights, she noticed from the corner of her eye a plain white sheet of paper, folded in half and tossed on her dashboard.

With a shiver, Nancy remembered all the anonymous notes she'd seen lately. A vision of Annie Mercer's demented scrawl flashed in her memory. Nervously, she picked up the note. With one eye on the road, she flipped the paper open.

Dear Nan,
    Sometimes it's hard for me to tell you these things in person. I wasn't very under-

standing when you were trying to solve this case. I accused you of not having faith in me, when I didn't have faith in you. Can you forgive me?

Glancing up at the road, Nancy whispered to herself, Yes, Ned, of course I forgive you. Then she read on:

I know the answer is yes, because I know you love me. And you'd better come back to Emerson soon, so I can show you how much I love you, too.

With all my heart,
Ned

Nancy's next case:

Bess has landed a job at the Razor's Edge dance club, and she's invited Nancy along to see what the excitement's about. It's a real scene: a wild young crowd, crazy costumes, a handsome DJ spinning the tunes— the kind of place where anything can happen. And it soon does. First, the blackout. Followed by a scream. Then the shocking discovery: Bess has disappeared!

Nancy takes the lead in a desperate search for her missing friend. The evidence all points to kidnapping, but suddenly the investigation takes an even darker turn. One of her prime suspects in the case—the gorgeous DJ—is found dead, strangled in his apartment. The party may be over . . . but Nancy's dance with danger is only beginning . . . in *Dance Till You Die,* Case #100 in The Nancy Drew Files™.

THE HARDY BOYS® CASEFILES